JAN 31 2019

# Broken Beasts
### *Book Three of the Xoe Meyers Series*
Sara C. Roethle

D1444650

Broken Beasts

The third book in the Xoe Meyers
Fantasy/Horror Series Copyright ©2013 by Sara
C. Roethle
First Printing: July 27th, 2013
Young Adult Fantasy/Horror
Published by Vulture's Eye Publications.

Manufactured in the United States of America

### *Dedication*
*To Sarah and Heather, for sticking by me and supporting me a ridiculous amount. Also, they edited this book, so if you find mistakes, blame them.*

**ACKNOWLEDGEMENTS**

Thanks to Melissa for being my beautiful cover model. Thanks to Dee, Audrey, and the rest of our super secret girl group for being awesome and supportive always. Thanks to the fam, always and forever. And lastly, thanks to Jesse, for being the best partner in crime and life that money can buy. Not that I bought him, but if manfriends could be bought, I'd drop every penny I had on him.

# Chapter One

Standing in line at the airport. So this was what it had all come down to. Jason was standing to my left, and Chase to my right. They are polar opposites except for their height. At 6'2" Jason is slightly taller than Chase's 6', but the similarities end there. Where Jason has brown hair, blue eyes, and lighter skin, Chase has black hair, dark gray eyes, and darker skin. I'm a pasty ghost compared to either of them with my blonde hair, green eyes, and white-as-a-sheet complexion.

Jason and Chase had become like my own personal bodyguards since the abduction incident . . . extremely annoying, but fairly cute bodyguards. I could hear Chase softly humming. I'd had about enough of his damn humming. It was never something normal. Today it sounded like the *Harry Potter* theme.

Just about a month ago, some wannabee

supernaturals had kidnapped me with the intention of stealing my powers. When I say wannabee, I mean that they wanted to be like other supernaturals, so they were killing them in an attempt to steal their powers. I'm a half-demon by the way, so is the boy to my right, well, he's a little more than half. The other boy is a vampire. And let's not forget the werewolves standing in line behind us. They were the reason I was at the Portland, Oregon airport preparing to fly down South to Moab, Utah.

See, amongst the chaos of kidnappings, new "friends", and the reappearance of my long-lost father, I'd managed to become the leader, or "alpha" of a misfit werewolf pack.

Now we were all on our way to meet with the Werewolf Coalition. That's right, the werewolves actually have a governing body, a place for every wolf, and every wolf in their place. If we wanted to have our place, we had to prove ourselves. I'd been trying to not think too hard on what proving ourselves might entail.

I held Jason and Chase's tickets as well as my own. When we reached the front of the line, the female security guard took the tickets with a smirk and a raised eyebrow. I gave her a dirty look and shoved Chase forward to walk first through the metal detector.

"Thanks Darling," Chase jested, his slight accent that I was yet to place coloring his words. I guess I could just ask him what it was, but Chase didn't like to talk about his past.

Jason chuckled and walked through next. The security guard could speculate all she wanted, she *so* did not know the most interesting things about us.

Jason hadn't quite managed a friendship with Chase over the past month, but he at least tolerates him now. They seem to have some sort of understanding between them. Chase looks out for me because my dad asked him to, and Jason because he's my boyfriend. If they were logical, they'd understand that they both have the same end goal and go from there, but when are boys really logical?

We turned and waited for Lucy and Max to walk through the detectors. Lela and Allison had gone to Utah a few days ahead of us to fill out paperwork and get our rooms at one of the local inns situated.

Question: Why did we need Allison there when she had nothing to do with werewolf affairs?

Answer: We didn't.

We had all agreed that it would be best if she didn't come. She's human, and there was no need for her to put herself in danger. Despite our

3

decision, Allison had caught up with Lela, telling her that she was supposed to go with her. We'd found out because Lela had called to check in and had mentioned Allison.

Now Lela, for some reason, holds the firm belief that I plan on beating her up when I get to Utah. I have no intention of doing so . . . probably. I was annoyed, but one does not simply get into fistfights with werewolves over a little annoyance.

My cell phone rang as we were waiting for the security lady to search Max's bags. I still have an old crappy flip phone. No fancy phones for this girl. I suppose it would be convenient to have one, but when you accidentally set things on fire a lot, carrying around expensive electronics becomes impractical.

I checked the screen to see that it was my mom . . . again. She had grudgingly let me go to Utah, as long as I promised I wouldn't get behind in school. She's still trying to cope with finding out that her only child is part demon. She has accepted it somewhat. She had known for years that my dad was something . . . other, but she didn't know he was a demon until I'd found out myself and told her.

It had actually been Chase that talked her into letting me go, with the promise that he would look after me. She loves Chase, don't ask me why. She knows he's a demon, just like she knows what the rest of us are, but for some reason it doesn't seem to bother her. I silenced the phone and shoved it back into my pocket.

As soon as Max had put his shoes back on, we headed for our gate. Lucy was the only one of our group that minded flying, as far as I knew. I'm pretty sure that her fear springs from her obsessive need to be in control of everything. I glanced at her petite figure as she tensely walked like there was something shoved in a place I won't mention, and decided to keep my theory to myself.

We sat to wait for boarding and I instantly pulled out my copy of Vonnegut's *Cat's Cradle*. Feeling the worn pages in my grasp was an instant comfort. I'm one of those weirdos that will reread a book multiple times. I find it's like watching a favorite movie, you learn the words so well that you can open the book and pick up anywhere in the story and still enjoy it.

It would have probably been smart to discuss the matters at hand with the group. We were, after all, heading towards a gathering of werewolves. We also weren't really sure what would be expected of us. A more in-depth game plan would have been nice, but I was fine with just reading instead.

We'd discussed our own opinions on how we should handle this little trip to the point of redundancy, and I didn't plan on giving anyone the opportunity to discuss it with me further. I just wanted to get it over with.

We didn't have to wait long. The slow process of boarding began. Apparently we'd made it just in time. If we had been much later we might have missed our flight. That would be terrible. That was sarcasm there, if you didn't catch it.

I haven't flown much, but I've been told that it's best to get to the airport at least an hour before your flight. That had been my plan, but try telling that to a frantic new werewolf about to meet a whole slew of her own kind.

Lucy had never really cared much about her style, but apparently the situation made clothing a lot more important in her mind. Add in her extremely over-protective mother and her extremely talkative little sister, and well . . . we didn't have to wait long at the airport.

I managed to keep my nose in my book the entire time we waited in the slowly shuffling line that led us onto the aircraft. As soon as we were on the plane, I quickly snagged the only window seat in our block of tickets.

The plane had three seats on each side of the isle. Lucy and Max slid into the two seats beside me, leaving Chase and Jason to share a row with a rather large man already sitting in the window seat.

I cringed at the smell of recycled airplane air, then buckled my seat belt and raised my book back up in front of my face. I glanced over at Lucy, but she didn't see me. Her eyes were shut tight in concentration, probably counting to ten over and over again in her head.

She didn't even notice as a young girl in a school uniform tried to shove her suitcase in the overhead compartment for our group of seats. The girl couldn't quite reach, and nearly dropped the suitcase on Lucy's head before an adult finally helped her out.

The steward gave us the whole safety spiel, and I finally started getting a little nervous. What if someone on the plane made me mad and I started a fire? If it could happen with TVs and washing machines, what was to stop me getting angry and exploding one of the plane's engines? Maybe I should just try to sleep the whole flight.

I glanced over at Jason, who gave me a smile and a thumbs up. Chase had already managed to procure a pillow and blanket from the stewardess. I was pretty sure they didn't usually hand those things out until after takeoff. I gave him a considering look, and he mimicked

Jason's thumbs up with two of his own. I turned back around as the plane started moving forward on the runway. A deep breath and away we went.

# Chapter Two

The flight was thankfully uneventful. When we arrived, Lela was waiting at the small airport for us with a very large, black SUV. The back had two rows of seats so we could all fit in one trip. Lela refused to make any eye contact with me while we loaded our luggage into the back of the SUV. I felt a twinge of satisfaction at having a tall, exotic knock-out afraid of me. Petty, who me?

We were able to slide all of our luggage into the trunk space without having to stack anything. This was a nod to the amount of trunk space, and not to our minimal luggage, because it wasn't minimal at all. We had packed for all contingencies, not knowing what type of clothing would be appropriate for meeting the other wolves.

"Okay," I announced, "Who wants the front seat?"

"You have to take it," Lela interjected, finally flipping her long dark hair out of her face. "You're Alpha. You can't sit in the back."

Oh, more werewolf etiquette; joy. Feeling crankier than ever, I asked, "What happens if you have more than two Alphas in the same car."

Lela opened the front door and looked at me meaningfully. "They fight."

"Who's going to know if I ride in the back?" I pushed.

Lela gave me a very serious look. "They'll know. They always do."

I got in without another word. This was so not my idea of a vacation. Everyone else piled in, much more somber than before. Lela got in the driver's seat and started the engine. We pulled out of the lot and onto a narrow highway.

Though there are still tall trees in Moab, its color scheme was something completely foreign to me, having grown up in Oregon. Cliff faces formed out of porous rock in shades of red, orange, and brown decorated the landscape at random intervals.

From what I could see the trees were mostly oak, but we had oak in Oregon too, only our oaks were surrounded by plenty of pine trees. The landscape was so visually stunning, that I managed to turn my thoughts to absorbing the scenery the entire drive to our destination. With the amount of pending thoughts to process, it was quite a feat.

Our hotel was a quaint little inn with red paint to match the orange and red rock surroundings. We got out of the SUV and walked onto the asphalt. The perfectly manicured lawn hosted a slew of people waiting in front of a table to get what looked like ID badges.

Noticing my interest, Lela dug in her large leather purse and produced a handful of lanyards with our names on them.

"One of the reasons I got here early," she explained. "We're all signed in and ready to go. Plus, the latecomers had to get rooms at a different hotel after the inn filled up. This way we won't have to drive to get to any of the meetings."

"The meetings are all at the inn?" Lucy asked walking up behind us, quickly taking everyone's lanyards from Lela. That's our Lucy, always straight to business.

"No," Lela answered, forming a smirk with her full lips. She gestured her hand in a sweeping motion to the wooded area behind the inn, "they're held out there."

Well that wasn't ominous at all. I felt

hands on my shoulders and leaned back against Jason's chest. He has a way of always knowing when I'm stressed. Jason moved to put one arm around my shoulders, and guided me in the direction of the inn. I'm tall for a girl, but Jason is tall for a guy, so he can comfortably put his arm over my shoulders.

My feet didn't seem to want to move. I had one lovely moment of keeping my tattered gray sneakers glued to the ground, then I had no choice but to walk into the wolf den, with my pack of wolves behind me.

Before we could reach the door of the inn, one of the last people I wanted to see came walking up. Abel is tall, dark, and handsome; either Hispanic or more likely American Indian, though he has no accent that I can decipher either way. Today his long dark hair was pulled back into a tight braid that trailed over his shoulder. I felt the sudden urge to yank that braid out of his skull, or maybe set it on fire. I resisted the urge . . . barely.

Abel hadn't actually done anything wrong as far as me and mine were concerned, but I couldn't help blaming him for this debacle anyway. He's the leader of the Western sector of the Werewolf Coalition, and this whole mess had begun because the lot of them hadn't put down a very crazy werewolf.

Said crazy werewolf had scratched my best friend, turning her into a werewolf, and the downward spiral went on from there. So yeah, Abel didn't *really* do anything wrong, but he didn't do anything right either, and a girl's gotta have an outlet for her anger.

Abel came to stand in front of us. Jason stepped back to give me room. Abel came eye to eye with Jason's tall frame. I was left to stare at the silver buttons on his rather tight fitting black vest. There was no shirt underneath.

Lela stood directly behind me. Her attempt at hiding would have been more effective if she weren't an inch or two taller than me. A fleeting thought brushed through my mind that Lucy and Max must feel like they're hanging out with a bunch of giants all the time.

Abel spoke, interrupting my thoughts. "So glad that you are here Alexondra. I've promised your father that I will do my best to return you to him in your current state."

The double meaning wasn't lost on me. My current state wasn't the best, considering what a mess my life was. Still, I took Abel at his word. My dad's a demon. Breaking a promise to him would probably be bad. I still didn't feel any safer though.

"It's Xoe," I grumbled in response. "And let's hope you're good at keeping your

13

promises."

He smiled. "I assure you I am. I trust your flight went well."

"Sure," I replied tartly. "Don't you have other guests to greet?"

Ok normally I'm not *that* rude, but I was in defense mode. I was in a new place that I didn't want to be in, and I was soon to be surrounded by new people I didn't want to be surrounded by. My go-to defense was grumpy. Anyone that got in my way would be showered by a torrential downpour of grumpy.

Abel chuckled. "This should be interesting."

With that cryptic observation, Abel turned away and moseyed towards the lanyard supply table. His black jeans fit as tightly as his vest. Men should simply not wear pants that tight. His black boots blended into his jeans so that at a distance you couldn't tell where one started and where the other ended.

"You're staring," Chase whispered in my ear.

Crap, it probably seemed like I'd been staring at Abel's butt. I guess I had. Not in admiration mind you. I made a mental note to always keep my eyes on the ground when I'm lost in thought, and headed towards the inn door, trying to hide my blush.

Chase chuckled and walked ahead to hold the door for me. He gave me a little salute as I walked through the doorway. Had I mentioned that this was going to be a long trip? Well, what I meant was that this was going to be a very, very, very, long trip.

By the time we pushed through the crowd in the lobby and got to our rooms it was already 5:00pm. We had two rooms, one with two beds and a cot, and the other with just two beds. Lucy and Allison were going to share a bed in the smaller room. My options were to share with Lela in the girls' room, or share with Jason in the boys' room. I ended up in the boys' room.

After examining the rustic room, complete with Terracotta pots and paintings of desert scenes with horses, I sprawled across the Southwestern themed comforter of Jason's and my rather small bed. Chase sat down on the cot with a sour expression on his face. He had lost to Max at rock, paper, scissors. The two of them didn't want to sleep in the same bed. Yet another example of boys being silly.

Chase bounced back and forth a bit on his cot, distaste showing plainly in his dark gray eyes. His near-black hair was starting to look a little shaggy, as opposed to that elegantly tousled look that some boys manage. He didn't really seem to care either way.

I twined my fingers through the ends of my own shaggy hair in thought. I still hadn't managed to find the time to get it cut. My demon lessons with my dad took up way more of my time than I liked. I was actually looking forward to a little vacation from him.

Going from not knowing my dad, to seeing him multiple times a week was overwhelming to say the least. I'd blamed him at first for not being in my life, but then I'd been enlightened of the fact that my mom had done her best to keep me away from him. I'd gotten over the hurt . . . mostly. He was definitely trying to make up for it now, in a really annoying way.

It wasn't all bad though. The lessons had definitely paid off. I was now able to manifest a small flame in my palm and could burn things on command, rather than on accident. It was peanuts compared to what my dad could do, but I'm just happy to finally have a measure of control. I don't randomly explode appliances anymore, but I for some reason can't do it voluntarily now either.

I looked down at the ring my dad had given me for Christmas, a family heirloom apparently. We didn't know what it did, if anything, but I've caught occasional flashes of light from the deep red stone. Sometimes even the silver vines that make up the band seemed to move, but whenever I tried to show anyone they stopped. The ring gave me the serious heebie-jeebies to tell the truth, but my dad insisted that I wear it. I'd given up on asking why.

Whenever my sense of teenage rebellion would flare up I'd take it off, but I always put it back on after a few hours. It would be seriously stupid if something bad happened, just because I didn't want to wear a ring. Of course, wouldn't it be even more stupid if something bad happened because I wore a ring out of fear of something bad happening? Don't answer that. For now, I'd wear the ring.

A quick knock on the adjoining door preceded Allison's entrance. I was still cranky with her for weaseling her way along on our trip. I was responsible for enough people already. I didn't need to be watching out for her too.

Allison's long, honey blonde hair was tied back in a tight ponytail, leaving her face completely unframed. It was a new look for her, and made her pale brown eyes look big and innocent. The smile she gave me was definitely not innocent. She was enjoying the fact that she had pulled one over on us. Bitter much?

She sat beside me in her designer jeans

and charcoal v-neck sweater, snapping the strap of my black spaghetti strap shirt on her way down.

"Aren't you freezing?" she asked, eyebrow raised.

"I'm always hot these days," I groaned in reply. "I feel like a human space heater."

Allison placed a hand against the side of my neck. Her palm felt cold and dry.

"You don't feel *that* warm. I mean yeah, you kind of feel like a human heating pad, but not uncomfortably so," she stated in a skeptical manner.

I glared at her. "Yes, I'm pleasantly warm to someone who's cold, but try feeling like you're standing in the sun twenty-four seven."

"Hey I've been wondering," Max piped in loudly from his perch on his bed, "we already know that you can't get burned by fires or hot surfaces, but can you get sunburned?"

The fact that I couldn't get burned by hot surfaces was a fairly recent discovery. The novelty had somewhat worn off. At first I'd amused myself by taking hot pans out of the oven without gloves and putting my hand in the fireplace, but it seemed to upset my mom, so I stopped. Well I stopped doing it while she was looking.

I hadn't yet considered the idea of the sun not being able to burn me. "I haven't managed it yet," I replied sullenly. "Considering the fact that before my powers came into action I would burn in about ten minutes, I'd say I probably don't need sunblock anymore."

I was feeling less and less human every day. Maybe I'd still wear the sunblock just to make myself feel better.

Max opened his mouth to say something else, but before he could, Allison stood abruptly and marched back into her room. She shut the door firmly behind her, as if she couldn't stomach another word from him.

I turned to give Max a suspicious look. "What did you do to make her mad?"

Max shrugged in reply. "I turned her down."

"Like for a date?" Chase interjected skeptically.

Max is 5'4" with sandy blond hair, pale green eyes, and freckles. I will forever think of him as a little elf. Allison on the other hand is 5'9", blonde, and curvy.

"Not for a date," Max said with more than a hint of venom, "though we have been on a few of *those*. She asked me to make her a wolf. I told her she was being an idiot and she got offended."

"What!" I exclaimed, jumping up from the bed. Oh, this was *so* not happening. I'd worked very hard to keep my last human friend out of the freak-show.

Max shrugged, as if it weren't a big deal. "She's tired of being the only human, but she doesn't understand what she's asking. I tried to explain it to her, but she wouldn't listen."

Oh, she was *tired* of being the only human, so why not just become a werewolf? I'd tell her why not. Maybe she wouldn't listen to Max, but I'd *make* her listen to me.

I turned from Max and marched straight into the girls' room without a knock. Allison was *lucky* to be the only human. I found her standing by the window talking to Jason. I brushed past him and shoved Allison down onto the nearest bed.

I jumped on top of her and pinned her down, my demon-fueled strength quickly putting an end to her struggles. I'm as strong as a werewolf when I'm angry, unfortunately I only have human strength when I'm not.

Werewolves have their strength all of the time. Being a werewolf changes the entire composition of someone's body. It's a magic of a sort, but more chemical. My strength was fueled by pure magic alone, and since I don't have much control of my magic, I don't have much control of my strength.

"Why are you here?" I demanded.

She looked to Jason for help, but he just raised his hands in surrender and backed away. I've always said he is a very smart man.

Allison turned her attention back to me with a defiant look in her eyes. I vaguely noticed that our entire party had filtered into the room, and everyone was huddled as far back from us as possible. Everyone, except for Chase that was. He's the only one I can't burn, something about a demon aura. Not that I hadn't tried a time or two. He can be rather infuriating when he wants to be. I could still set the room around Chase on fire, but I'd try to restrain myself.

I should have been exercising more caution around Allison. As the only human, if I burned her, she'd heal human slow. Everyone else in the room could take a beating . . . erm, burning. Allison couldn't. That thought alone helped me calm my anger a bit.

I focused all of my attention back on the human in question. "Why?" I demanded again.

"I don't want to be human anymore," she mumbled quickly. "Max and Jason both refused to help me."

I whipped my gaze up to regard Jason. "You knew?" I asked, shocked.

"I've been trying to talk her out of it," he replied, voice steady.

His aura of calm was given away by the fact that he couldn't seem to stop running his hands through his dark brown hair. It was his most obvious nervous tell. You'd think after all of the years he'd been alive he would have grown out of it, but old habits die hard.

I regarded the rest of the room, Allison nearly forgotten underneath me. "Who else knew?"

After a moment of silence, Lela raised her hand, but refused to lift her gaze from the floor. So she had asked everyone in our group except Chase, Lucy, and me . . . the only ones she knew couldn't, or wouldn't help her.

Being a demon is hereditary. It can't be passed on like lycanthropy. It's more difficult to make someone a vampire, they often die in the process, but it can be done. The fact that she'd asked Jason to turn her meant that she was desperate. Desperate and stupid.

I slowly crawled off of the bed and marched out into the hallway, instead of back into the other room. I shut the door behind me to signify that no one should follow me, then made my way downstairs and back outside. I'd been losing my temper like this a lot lately. Everyone knew to let me cool off. People ended up with blisters otherwise.

The lawn was still crowded with werewolves. I *so* did not want to see werewolves. I might set one of them on fire. Instead of walking through them, I made a quick left and headed straight out into the woods, not really knowing where I was going. I needed time to think.

After a good ten minutes of walking mindlessly, I finally began to take in my surroundings. The trees in this area were completely alien compared to those in Shelby. Everything in Moab was drier, and . . . spikier.

I had noticed that the river near the hotel supported towering cottonwood trees, but once you ventured away from the moisture it all became short, spine-covered mesquites and other unforgiving plant life.

The mountains in the near distance were populated with the same oaks I had noticed on our drive. Maybe I'd still see pines later tonight at the werewolf "meet and greet," which would take place in said mountains. Why on earth would Allison want to be part of this?

I mean, I know on the outside having powers and extra strength and speed seems cool . . . okay it's definitely kind of cool, but the drawbacks aren't worth it. Since I'd found out I was a demon, I had been kidnapped and beaten.

I'd been lied to and used. I'd hurt people. I'd *killed* people. My life was in constant disarray. My mom is afraid to even ask about my life anymore.

There will always be people wanting to use me, or hurt me. Whoever first said that power corrupts was right, though they probably didn't mean it in the sense that I'm using it. Power corrupts your life when you have it and other people want it.

Allison knew everything that Lucy and I had gone through since our lives were changed by paranormal means. She'd been there to see it all. Heck, she'd even gotten beaten and kidnapped herself, just for being near us. Voluntarily becoming a part of that world was just plain stupid. I couldn't let her do it. If she was too stupid to protect herself from our fate, then I'd do it for her. She wasn't becoming a werewolf. I'd have to see to that tonight.

# Chapter Three

Payback is a bitch. I was beginning to realize that werewolves don't like it when non-werewolves kill them. No matter that the werewolf I'd killed was psychotic and trying to kill me. I was even getting blamed for Nick's death, which was actually my dad's doing. Nick had also been trying to kill me.

As soon as I reached the Inn's lawn after my little reflective walk, an older woman, presumably a werewolf walked up and tried to spit on me. She missed, but I didn't. She hadn't taken into account that my powers were fueled by anger. I managed to knock her out with a single punch. Respect for my elders be damned. I stepped right over her prostrate form without another glance and kept walking.

Everyone else on the lawn stared at me as I made my way towards the front door of the Inn. Some faces held looks of fear or respect, but most only held hatred. Screw it. I wasn't here to win any popularity contests.

I met Lela in the hall as I was walking back to our room. "What's with all of the hostility around here?" I asked bluntly.

She just stood there uncomfortably, obviously not wanting to answer my question. Instead she focused on tugging her black sweater down over her jeans, as if it didn't already fit her perfectly.

I raised my eyebrow at her and she stopped fidgeting.

"Basically," she began, "No one likes you, because you're involved in werewolf affairs, but you aren't a werewolf yourself. No one likes the rest of us, because we'd rather be led by a demon than one of our own."

"So why am I even here?" I asked. "I was under the impression that this was for the good of all of us."

Lela had stopped fidgeting. She was all business now. One of the reasons I liked her was that when she had a purpose, she got things done. One of the reasons I didn't like her was that when she didn't have a purpose, she was a crying mess looking for someone to take care of her.

Luckily, right now she had it together. "It *is* good for all of us. If it works it will offer us all a great deal of protection, but the fact still stands that the only reason we were even allowed to be a pack is that Abel for some reason pushed our paperwork through." She explained. "When you have the leader of an entire sector pushing for you . . . well you get pushed."

I was well aware that Abel had been pushing for us, it was the why that I was fuzzy on. As far as I could tell, Abel liked us . . . and I didn't trust that one little bit. I just wasn't that likeable.

"Why do you think he did it?" I asked, suspicion clear in my voice.

She shrugged. "I'm guessing something to do with your dad. It seems like they have a lot of history." She smiled a half-smile. "Maybe he's just bored."

I was a seventeen year old, out of state and completely out of my league, all because of a werewolf's boredom . . . how comforting.

I pulled my phone out of my pocket to check the time. Almost 6:00. High time to get ready and get the evening over with.

I took a deep breath and turned back to Lela. "Ok, tell me about this evening. What do we have to wear and what do we have to do?"

Lela's eyes flicked around the room nervously. "We don't have to *do* much . . . but, we kind of have to dress up. Evening meetings for the whole group are formal. Morning meetings for the Alphas are mostly informal."

I shook my head and smiled. If wearing formal wear was the worst thing I had to do, I could deal. Why did I have the sneaking suspicion that dressing up was only the tip of the proverbial iceberg?

# Chapter Four

Within an hour we had all marched back downstairs in our evening finery, which was seeming increasingly impractical as we tromped towards the meeting place in the middle of the woods.

I had been harangued into purchasing a crimson strapless dress that ended just below my knees in preparation for the occasion. It was nice and simple except for the fact that it was made of silk. The bodice was fitted, kind of corset style, but had no other embellishments to speak of.

The dress had cost a sizable chunk of the money I was awarded after the Dan incident. If anyone spit on it I would set their hair on fire, even though I'd probably never wear it again anyhow.

Lela was in black again, chic and simple with her hair twisted back in a simple bun.

Lucy's deep purple dress had sheer cap sleeves with lots of sparkles that continued down onto the dress. It was *way* more flashy than Lucy's normal attire. Her heels were a shiny silver with more little sparkles set in the straps. Her black hair hung long and sleek, perfectly straight and shiny without any styling whatsoever.

I was the only girl without a coat. I was also the only girl not in heels. I could only be talked into so much. I didn't give a damn that my sneakers looked horribly out of place. I had four other dresses in garment bags in my closet. The sneakers would be worn with all of them. My hair was a scruffy looking mess like usual. I'd had a brief stint of actually styling it, but that had gotten old fast.

Jason looked rather snazzy beside me in charcoal dress pants and a shirt that was as dark as purple manages to get before it turns black. Someone had gotten Chase into a similar outfit but with black pants and a deep green shirt. They looked like they had been dressed to match.

As my two bodyguards I supposed it was appropriate. Lela had probably coordinated it. Heck, maybe she'd even bought the clothes for them. Jason could be pushed into shopping on occasion, but Chase would rather have his toenails pulled out then spend a day trying on clothes. I had expected Chase to look uncomfortable like me, but he actually wore his fancy attire quite well.

Why did Jason and Chase need to fit in, and why were they even allowed to come to the meeting? My dad had arranged it. My dad wanted me to have bodyguards, and Abel wanted me to have a werewolf pack. Thus, strings were pulled, and we were all on our way to our first werewolf meeting. Allison, despite her protests, was staying in the room.

We had exited the inn to a very surreal scene. Werewolves of all ages were dressed to the nines and making their way towards the woods. No one looked awkward in their heels. They all walked with an eerie, boneless grace. I would have looked awkward.

The only thing to mar their perfect appearance were the lanyards with each individual's information dangling around their necks. I had my lanyard in my hand, rather than around my neck. I wasn't really sure if I wanted everyone to know who I was on sight, plus I hate lanyards.

I noticed a few side-long glances as we converged with the crowd. I did my best to ignore them. Wouldn't do to get in another fistfight on our very first day amongst the werewolves. Noticing a few of the wolves nearing our group, Jason and Chase took their posts on either side of me. A young couple hesitated, then walked away, but a single man in an all-black suit continued towards us.

We had to walk directly at him to stay in the flow of wolves entering the woods, and I wasn't about to swerve aside for him, so within a minute we were face to face.

He was tall, but fell a few inches short of Jason and Chase. I placed him around 5'10". A polite smile flooded his clean-shaven face. He had a strong jaw and full lips, very GQ . . . or at least what I imagine GQ to be. Slicked back blond hair completed his overly manicured appearance. He looked young to be so well put together. I placed him at around twenty. He held out a hand to me.

I stared at the hand like it was road-kill, but then, not wanting yet another enemy, I placed my hand in his. He lifted my hand to his mouth and kissed it gently. Seriously? I fought to keep my discomfort off my face and failed.

I withdrew my hand, trying to hide my distaste.

Smile never faltering, he introduced himself. "I'm Devin. I presume you're Alexondra. I've heard so much about you."

What I wanted to say, was hi Devin, I've heard absolutely nothing about you. 'kay, bye, but what came out of my mouth was far more diplomatic. So diplomatic it made my teeth hurt.

"Nice to meet you Devin. Care to walk and talk? I don't want to get left behind." I gestured at the majority of the crowd disappearing in the distance.

"Why of course," he replied, holding out his suit clad arm for me to take.

In my experience that level of politeness meant either someone wanted something, or they were afraid of you. Devin didn't seem afraid, so the question was, what did he want? Ah well. With a shrug I placed my arm through his and began to walk towards the meeting place with the rest of my group trailing behind us. I thought I could almost sense Jason's discomfort, but maybe I was just projecting.

"You're warm," Devin commented. "It that because of your demon blood?"

I stumbled at his words, but recovered quickly and managed to not fall on my face.

Devin chuckled. "Come now Alexondra. You know what we all are. It's only fair that we know a bit about you."

"It's Xoe," I corrected, then asked, "You can feel my temperature through your coat?"

"Yes," he replied as we veered towards the mountains and the larger trees. "We wolves run slightly hotter than humans, but not enough to be easily perceptible. You're like a little heater."

I didn't like being called little. Sure I'm slightly scrawny, but I'm also tall. I prefer to think I'm a lot more imposing than I actually am. I almost protested the remark. Yet, I was trying to be polite, and I couldn't think of a reason not to tell him, so I answered his question instead.

"It has to do with the specific line of demons I come from. We have freakishly fast metabolisms. Though, whether the heat fuels our powers, or is an aftereffect of them, I'm not sure."

"Interesting," Devin replied. "So I'm told you can create fire, what else can you do?"

It took a moment for me to register what he had said. He'd managed to gather a lot more intelligence than I would have thought.

"Oh no," I replied. "That's all you get. A girl has got to maintain a bit of mystery."

Devin smiled and nodded at my answer, then went on to the next subject without a hitch. "Have you been told what to expect from this meeting?"

I shrugged. "Not really, you werewolves can be a bit cryptic. All I know is that formal wear is a must."

Devin's smile returned. "Well you've got

the formal wear down . . . except for the shoes, but there are a few more things you should know."

"And what are those things?" I prompted, getting impatient.

"You're petitioning to become a pack. There are many among us that will challenge your claims," he began.

Pssh, tell me something I didn't know. "Are you one of the challengers?" I asked. Subtlety is not my strong suit.

Devin shrugged gracefully. I've never managed the graceful shrug thing.

"I have a more casual interest in the matter," he answered. "A few of us have placed bets on the outcome."

I tried to pull my arm away from his, but he held on. "Don't worry Xoe," he soothed, "I'm on your side. I see no reason why you shouldn't become a pack. Plus, very few bet on you succeeding. I stand to win some serious cash."

"Lovely," I grumbled in response.

"Now don't be sore Xoe," Devin continued. "I was on your side even without the cash. These meetings can be so boring. We need a little excitement."

We had entered a clearing packed full of werewolves. A big group of them turned to glare at me. The woman who had tried to spit on me was at the front of that group.

"Happy to oblige," I told Devin, causing him to grin like the proverbial crocodile. I couldn't help the thought that grins like that tended to come back and bite you in the ass.

# Chapter Five

There was a space in the crowd which I assumed was for us. Devin led us over to that area, then finally let go of my arm. I expected him to weave through the crowd to find his group, but instead he went to stand by Abel in the center of the clearing. They were in cahoots. I should have known.

Jason took my arm that had been freed of Devin and led me to sit on a large rock in our part of the clearing. Glancing around, I realized that there were several large rocks that people were beginning to take their seats on. A few people ended up on the ground, but those of us in the front got rocks.

I looked back to see that the majority of the crowd wasn't even in the clearing at all. They stood amongst the trees. If I wasn't so against being there myself, I might have felt bad for their exclusion. As it was, I envied them.

I turned my attention back to my group, and realized that my group had diminished to just Chase, Jason, and me. Lela was shooing Max and Lucy back into the trees. I looked at Jason questioningly and he just shrugged apologetically.

Chase leaned in on my other side and whispered, "Only pack alphas in the center clearing."

"Then why are you and Jason still here?" I asked.

He shrugged. "Lela says."

I watched as the last few wolves filed themselves away into the woods, like smoke dissipating through the cracks. Their absence left fourteen distinct groups. I had expected more individual packs.

Each group had three to four wolves. From the way they were sitting, I guessed that the Alpha, and sometimes the Alpha's spouse were seated in front, all with two bodyguard types slightly behind them. I realized that Chase and Jason's rocks were slightly behind me. I guess Jason didn't qualify as my "spouse."

I guesstimated that there were about 50 figures standing in the woods now. That would mean 3-4 extra wolves per pack. I remembered Lela saying that the entire pack didn't have to attend the meetings each time, but we all had to be there to petition. I wondered how many members of the other packs weren't in attendance.

"Welcome," Abel boomed, drawing everyone's attention to him. He had kept the skintight pants, but had changed into a silken dress shirt the exact color of my dress. We were matching. He couldn't have planned it, there was just no way. Unless Lela had told him. The smile he gave me told me that it had most definitely been planned. Gre-eat.

"Let us get right down to business," Abel went on, drawing his gaze away from me. "Who will be the first to update?"

"We will," the woman who had tried to spit on me piped in. The black eye I had given her was already healing to a sickly yellow. Noticing my glance, she flipped a portion of her graying dirty-blond hair over her eye.

The man sitting beside her rose to his feet. He was built like a highly-muscled bear with salt-and-pepper hair. He tugged his striped dress shirt straight, like he wasn't used to dressing up. "What Greta means," he grumbled, "is that *I* will begin."

I sensed some marital strife there. Abel nodded and gestured for bear-man to begin. I got bored about two minutes into bear-man's speech. He went on and on about pack laws broken, and punishments doled out. It went much the same with the next group. It didn't seem like Abel was even listening as he sat on the biggest rock in the center of the clearing.

As the third group began their "updates," Devin came to crouch beside me. He leaned in way too close to me. I started to lean away, but realized he was trying to whisper in my ear. You had to whisper very softly around werewolves. Jason was close enough that with his vampire hearing, he'd probably hear everything that Devin whispered.

I held still as Devin practically kissed my ear, and whispered, "What updates will you present?"

I shrugged in response. We weren't even officially a pack yet. How were we supposed to have updates.

Devin looked more than a little worried at my response. Apparently this update thing was more important than it seemed. Suddenly the talking had stopped and everyone's attention was on me.

"Xoe," Abel prompted. "Updates please?"

When I didn't move, Devin pinched my leg. I jumped to my feet, sparing him a quick angry glare.

"Um . . . " I stammered. "No rules

broken, no punishments doled out."

"You killed Nick," Greta interrupted. "You killed one of us."

"Actually Greta," I practically spat her name out. "I didn't kill him, but even if I did, he had just finished telling me about how he was going to slit my throat and feed me to a demon. Oh, did I mention that he kidnapped me first and held me hostage in a crypt?"

"You're not even one of us," Greta countered. "You shouldn't be here."

"The woman is observant," I mocked. "Somebody give her a prize."

Greta stood and started towards me, face contorted with anger. She managed to avoid bear-man as he made a grab for her. Jason and Chase both moved in front of me, but there was no need.

Faster than my eyes could follow, Abel intercepted Greta and shoved her so hard that she went flying. Her flight was stopped short by a nearby oak tree that made a horrible cracking sound with the force of her impact. She fell to the ground and didn't move.

Bear-man simply rose, walked over, gathered up the crumpled Greta, and disappeared into the trees. Everyone else stood in complete silence.

Abel casually walked back into the

center of the clearing. He clapped his hands together and bared his perfect white teeth in a smile that looked more like a snarl. "Updates! Who's next?"

Devin grinned and patted my shoulder as he stood to go rejoin Abel. The leader of the next group stood and started rattling off small discretions and their accompanying punishments. Jason's nervous energy was giving me goosebumps and Chase looked positively green. It was good to know that I probably wasn't the only one who felt like maybe my stomach was going to force itself in its entirety out of my throat.

# Chapter Six

When updates finally finished there was food. And good thing, because I was starving. Then again, I was always starving. The more I worked on my powers, the more it upped my metabolism. I was hungry all the friggin' time.

Apparently during social/food time, we were supposed to disperse from our packs and get to know each other a little better. Jason got led away by Devin. It had been agreed upon earlier that either Chase or Jason would stay with me, so Chase simply refused to leave my side whenever someone tried to draw him or I away from each other.

When we were alone I glared up at him, "I can take care of myself you know."

"Of course," Chase conceded. "Let's get some food."

"But-" I began to argue. Chase put his arm around my shoulders and turned me to face the food table that had been brought in towards the end of updates.

"Oh fine," I gave in, seeing the spread of miniature sandwiches, cakes, and all sorts of fancy hors d'oeuvres. I walked out of Chase's arm and made a beeline for the table, with him catching up quickly behind me.

Chase stayed behind me, almost-touching, the entire time I gathered food. I could feel the line of his body about an inch away from my back.

I turned around and raised an eyebrow at him. "I'm not going to disappear you know."

He looked a question at me.

"Do you have to stand so close?" I clarified.

Chase had the courtesy to look embarrassed. "Sorry," he mumbled, and took a small step back.

"Don't you want anything?" I asked. "We haven't eaten since before our flight."

"Just throw me a few sandwiches on your plate?" he asked in return.

Without question, I added four more mini-sandwiches to the four I already had. It was lucky that the plates were big, even stacking everything up, all the food I grabbed wouldn't have fit on a normal size plate. Chase grabbed us each a bottle of water and we headed to the edge of the clearing away from the crowd. Screw being social.

I sat so I could lean my back against a truly massive oak tree. Chase sat cross-legged in front of me, and I placed the food plate on the ground between us.

Chase looked at me like he wanted to say something, but was going to bite his tongue and stay quiet. He started to hum under his breath.

I sighed. "Quit with the dam humming and spit it out."

Chase smiled ruefully. "You could have been a bit more diplomatic back there."

"Why should I?" I questioned petulantly. "It's not like Greta was trying too hard."

"Greta isn't trying to establish a werewolf pack," Chase argued.

I frowned. "I thought you didn't want me to have a werewolf pack. 'Needless danger' you called it."

Chase frowned back. "I'd rather you not get involved in werewolf affairs, but now that you have, things could go very badly."

I picked up one of our untouched sandwiches and took a bite. "Elaborate," I demanded, mouth full of crumbs.

Chase picked up a sandwich, but didn't eat. "You have a lot of enemies here Xoe. If your petition to form a pack is rejected, you won't be protected under pack law."

I dropped my sandwich back on the plate. How had I not thought of that? I'd just strolled on in like nothing could touch me.

I couldn't think of a proper reply, so I just said, "Oh."

"Yes Xoe. *Oh*," Chase went on, his accent emphasizing the *oh*. "You need to start thinking things through a little better."

"Like the guy who aligned himself with a rag-tag group of supernaturals?" I questioned. "All because you owe my demon dad some type of life debt? I'm sure that was well planned. And coming here? Will your debt ever end?"

"I don't owe him a life debt," Chase replied sharply. "He saved my life. Watching over you is the least I can do."

"I don't need you to *watch me*," I replied sharply. "I have plenty of other people to *watch me*. I don't even need watching!"

"Yes you do," Chase grumbled. "If anything happened to you, your dad would-"

"So that's the only reason you're still around?" I interrupted. "Because you think my dad would blame you if you left and something happened to me?"

"No!" he shouted in exasperation, drawing a few stares. Lowering his voice, he continued, "You know that's not the only reason I'm here Xoe."

I clutched my water bottle, anger and hurt commingling rather than trying to win out over one another. I just stared at him, not sure whether to apologize, or throw my bottle at him.

At that moment, Max came trotting up and plopped down beside me, grabbing a sandwich from our forgotten plate.

"This is actually kind of cool," Max said, not picking up on the tension. "It's so weird going from being completely alone, to knowing and getting to know so many other people like me."

Chase and I both stared at the ground in silence.

"Uh oh," Max said in a sing-song voice. "What did I miss?"

"Nothing," Chase mumbled as he stood and dusted himself off.

Max turned to me questioningly.

"Nothing," I agreed, and grabbed my forgotten sandwich.

Lucy walked up and sat with us as Chase walked away. "What's his problem?" she asked.

"Nothing," I repeated.

"Yes, you keep on saying that," Max observed, "but all signs point to something."

Lucy frowned. "What did he say to you

Xoe?"

I sighed loudly. "Nothing okay?"

I stood to leave . . . on second thought, I crouched back down and grabbed the food plate, shoving my water bottle underneath my arm. "I just need some air," I announced.

As I walked away I heard Max say, "But we're outside . . ."

Shaking my head, I continued walking, no destination in mind. Jason would be mad at me for going off alone, but screw it. I could take care of myself. I munched my sandwiches, which I now had way too many of, considering Chase had abandoned his share.

What was with him anyhow? Half the time he was a fun-to-be-around friend, the other half he was all broody. And yes, brooding can be cute, but it can also be very annoying.

All of the sudden Devin appeared at my side, causing me to jump and spill my food everywhere. All of my cute little sandwiches bounced into the dirt.

"Thanks," I said, handing him my empty plate as I continued walking.

He took it without hesitation and fell into stride beside me. "You shouldn't be walking around alone out here Xoe," he lectured. "Abel wanted me to make sure you don't get eaten."

"I have enough people watching over

me," I snapped back. "Trust me."

"So what's the deal with you and the other demon?" Devin questioned, ignoring my comment.

I stopped walking mid-stride and gave him a very annoyed look. "There is no deal," I said sharply. "He works for my dad."

He raised his hands in surrender. "Just curious, no offense meant."

I nodded and continued walking again.

"So . . . " he went on. "You're with the vampire then."

I sighed. "Yes, I'm with the vampire."

"Because it looked like-" Devin began, but stopped when he saw my glare.

"Why do you care anyhow?" I asked sharply.

Devin shrugged. I was tired of all of these men shrugging artfully at me. A real answer would be nice for a change.

As if reading my mind, Devin explained, "My place in this little microcosm is held because I know the correct information. I'd be a fool if I didn't continue to gather it."

I stopped walking to stare at him. "And why, pray tell," I asked, "is my relationship status important information?"

"For those that don't want to step on your toes," he began, "knowing who you're with will help them to avoid doing so. This information is even more pertinent to those who would stomp all over your little feet, given the opportunity."

I glared at him. "So what, you're trying to find out my weaknesses, so you can barter with the information?"

Devin shrugged again. "Or perhaps, I just want to make sure I don't step on your toes."

I snorted. "You're doing a bang up job there champ. I think I might end up losing a toenail."

I turned to keep walking, and much to my chagrin, he followed.

"I came out here alone for a reason, you know, because I wanted to be . . . alone," I said.

"Well since you're so into motives," he replied. "You can read into mine now, and deduce that I want the rest of your pack to like me too. Therefore I'm looking out for you, since you so carelessly ran away from your bodyguards whilst in a rather hostile environment."

"You know, you're right," I countered. "I should go find my bodyguards. I'd much rather be in that hostile environment, than out here walking with you."

I turned around to walk back in the

direction we'd come from, but stopped short at the sight of Jason speeding towards me.

Jason grabbed me into a hug as soon as he reached us, then held me out at arm's length to give me steady eye-contact. "I could kill Chase," he explained. "You're not supposed to be alone."

"I'm not," I replied, freeing one of my arms to give Devin a slap on the chest. "I've got good ol' Devin watching over me. Everyone is watching over me."

Jason crinkled his eyebrows, confused at my anger.

"I'll leave you two to it," Devin announced before quickly making his escape.

Jason kept his focus on me, his face still showing signs of confusion. "What's wrong? What happened?"

I sighed and shook my head. "I really wish people would stop asking me that. I just wanted to go for a walk."

"It's too dangerous for you to be alone right now Xoe," Jason lectured.

"Isn't it always?" I mumbled as the rest of our group came trotting up to us.

"There's a dance tonight," Lucy announced proudly.

"Seriously?" I questioned. "Is this like, junior high summer camp or something?"

Lucy frowned and playfully hit me on the shoulder. "C'mon Xoe, we're here, we may as well have fun with it."

"And dancing became fun when?" I asked.

Lucy sighed. "It's always been fun." She reached out and grabbed my hand before I could protest. "Let's go get ready."

I didn't have it in me to fight her. Weren't we already dressed up? Was pack meeting dressed-up somehow different from dance dressed-up? Did I care? Whatever.

I'd had too many realizations/enlightenments today. Chase had a lot that he wasn't telling me. We were at a werewolf summer camp. People wanted to kill me. Dancing has always been fun.

Most of these things I could believe, but dancing? Surely not.

# Chapter Seven

"I'm coming, end of story."

"No you're not," I assured.

"You, Xoe, would deny me a dance? I live for this kind of thing."

"The point Allison," I argued, "is that I want you to live."

Allison sighed. "I don't want to *die* Xoe. I just want to be a werewolf."

I glared at her. "You tried to become a vampire too. You really could have died in that process. Is it really worth dying over?"

Allison glared back. "It's my life Xoe. It's my choice."

"I'll make you a deal," I offered. "You can come with us to the dance, and any other fun activities, and I'm using the term fun very loosely here. You can come with us if you agree to wait on deciding to become a werewolf until after we get home."

"And how will I get someone to turn me once we're home?" She questioned.

I sighed. "You'll get to come out and meet all of the other werewolves. I'm sure you'll make some friends. You can seem charming to those who don't know any better."

She held out her hand to me without a second thought. "Deal."

We shook on it. No, I had not resigned myself to the idea of her becoming a werewolf. I would simply wait until we got home, then I'd lock her in a closet. Forever. Okay, maybe it wasn't the best plan, but at least this way I'd have time to think of something else. Maybe with time, she'd realize how ridiculous she was being. Yeah, and then we'd all ride away on our unicorns.

With our agreement out of the way, it was on to the horrible task of getting ready. I was in the girls' room with Lucy, Allison, and Lela. The boys were in the other room "getting ready," which meant watching TV and hogging the food from the complimentary gift basket that had been left waiting in our room.

Chase had given me the peace offering of some freshly gathered mini sandwiches when we had first gotten back to the room. It was a small consolation to him ruining our impromptu picnic, but it was a welcome one. Food was definitely the way to my heart.

Lucy and Lela were sharing the bathroom mirror, which left me all alone and at the mercies of Allison. She was pawing through my clothes, but the only dress she liked was the one I had worn to the earlier event. I probably should have been offended, but I didn't care. Personal style wasn't really my strong suit, and I was okay with that.

Slamming my suitcase shut, she marched over to the closet. I glanced inside to see that she had a row of garment bags already hung up with several pairs of shoes on the floor. She unzipped one of the bags and nodded her approval. Without looking, she crooked her finger at me to gesture that I should come to the closet.

I almost didn't do it, but I wanted Allison to keep her promise. I hadn't even reached the closet when she threw the garment bag at me and focused her attention on her selection of shoes. I laid the garment bag on the nearest bed and slowly unzipped it, dreading what was inside.

A medium length, jewel-green dress with delicate beading at the neck stared back at me. I removed it from the bag to find that the part that was supposed to cover my back was composed of a few thin strings of the same tiny, glittering beads that decorated the front. The dress had a high halter neck, so at least it wouldn't slip off.

I threw the dress back on the bed. "No way Al. Absolutely not."

Ignoring me, Allison walked over to the bed holding a pair of silver strappy sandals. Silver strappy sandals with four-inch heels.

My instincts screamed at me to run, which I wouldn't be able to do once I put the shoes on. I looked down at the offending footwear. "You realize you're asking me to risk my life with those?"

Allison smiled the wicked smile she always wears when she gets to dress me up. "You'll be fine Xoe. You're lucky you wear the same size shoe as me . . . enjoy it."

She dropped the shoes into my waiting hands and walked away towards the bathroom, no doubt to observe and critique Lucy's makeup. I looked down at the dress again. May as well get it over with.

I checked to make sure that the adjoining door to the boys room was locked and slipped out of my crimson dress. I still didn't see why I had to wear a whole new dress when I'd only worn the other one for a few hours. I struggled with the stringy non-straps of the new dress, being careful not to pull them too hard. When I finally got the thing pulled up and zipped, I went and did a quick twirl in front of the mirror above the room's generic desk.

The dress actually fit like a glove, and looked far less skanky than I thought it would. The neckline was cut high enough to balance out the revealing back. I instantly knew that Allison had brought it for me, with how tight it was on me, it never would have fit over her curves.

I humored myself with another twirl. The dress would work. The shoes on the other hand, I was still not sold on. I grudgingly put them on and walked around the room feeling like a newborn baby horse.

Allison exited the bathroom long enough to grab my hand and pull me back in with her. I clomped after her nearly spraining my ankle several times along the way.

The bathroom was rather spacious inside, especially compared to the size of the rest of the inn. Allison patted the gold-veined marble counter-top in-between the double sinks. With a grimace, I hopped up onto the counter to sit in front of her. I was pleased to find that I could at least sit in the dress comfortably.

Allison grabbed her makeup bag from the counter and observed my face like an artist looking at a blank canvas. I knew I'd have to go without concealer, since Allison, Lucy, and Lela are all darker than me. I wasn't about to cry over it.

The first thing she grabbed out of her bag of tricks was eyeliner, and I cringed. Putting eyeliner on yourself is scary enough, having someone else shoving a stick towards your eyes is downright nerve-wracking. I fidgeted so much while she tried to do it that she finally had to have me sit with my back and the back of my head against the wall so I couldn't pull away from her. She finally smudged enough on to make her happy, then she tortured me with mascara as well.

When she finally finished, Allison instructed me to look it over in the mirror. I appreciated that she hadn't gone overboard. The dark gray eyeliner was way more than I was used to, mainly since no makeup was what I was used to, but overall I could deal. The shoes still had to go.

A knock resounded at the adjoining door. I took my cue to escape the bathroom and ran (as much as one can run in four-inch heels) to unlock and open the door.

It was Jason, and he stopped dead in his tracks. He gave me the once-over while I waited patiently. The second once over elicited foot tapping on my part.

"Well?" I huffed.

"Woah," was the only reply I got.

Max walked past Jason into the room, then stopped and turned to me. "Woooah," he grinned, then turned to high-five Jason.

I walked back towards the bathroom. "That's it, I'm changing."

Allison met me at the door to the bathroom and forced me back out into the bedroom. "No way Xoe. Our deal includes me getting to dress you."

I tried to push past her, but I couldn't seem to get much traction in the heels. "Oh no, we never agreed on that."

"It was totally implied!" she exclaimed.

Suddenly I was lifted up and carried back to the center of the bedroom. Jason set me down and turned me to face him. "You look lovely Xoe. We didn't mean to embarrass you."

I looked at Max with a raised eyebrow.

He grinned back at me. "I totally meant to embarrass you, but if you must know, you look fantastic. Tall, but fantastic."

Chase finally came into the room to see what all of the commotion was. He spared me any comments. He simply smiled and did his best to not look me up and down. At least he was back to meeting my eyes again.

Allison came to stand in front of me with crossed arms. She tsk-ed under her breath.

"Now what am I going to do with you hair?"

I shrugged. "Leave it?"

She held up a finger gesturing for me to wait where I was and disappeared into the bathroom. She re-emerged with hairspray, a brush, and a little cardboard tab of bobby pins. Crap.

When she finished, my hair was in a loose up-do, with little braids twisted in and strands of hair falling strategically around my face.

When I finally escaped her, I went to sit next to Max on the bed to wait on the rest of the girls to get ready. Chase and Jason stood leaning against the wall looking bored out of their minds. The three boys were all still wearing their clothes from earlier. Being a girl is *so* not fair.

"We should have a signal," Max stated suddenly.

I turned and eyed him suspiciously. "Go on," I prompted.

"We should have a signal," he explained, "so we can alert each other whenever we need to be rescued from a dance, or a conversation. Some of the people here are a little intense."

Chase chuckled.

"Okay, what happened?" I asked, searching for an explanation.

Max began to blush.

Chase grinned a little wider, baring his teeth. "Max has an . . . admirer."

I laughed and turned back to Max. "Tell me. Is she hot?"

Max paled. "She's twelve."

"What!" I shouted. Taken aback. "Is she a werewolf?"

"Apparently," Max answered, "lycanthropy can be transmitted from a mother to her child. It makes sense I guess, since it's in the blood."

I paled. "Holy crap, a baby werewolf?"

Max shook his head. "I asked about her. Children born with lycanthropy don't turn the first time until they're ten or so."

"Uh," I began. "A ten year old werewolf is still pretty bad."

Max nodded. "Which is why she's mainly just been raised around her own kind. She's been pretty sheltered."

I smiled again, I couldn't help it. "So a twelve year old, sheltered werewolf has a crush on you?"

Max sighed loudly in response.

The whole idea was too creepy for words. Not a little girl's crush, but the way the little girl had been forced to live.

I patted Max on the shoulder. "I'll do my

best to save you from the little werewolf if you want, or you could just be nice and dance with her. She's probably pretty lonely without any friends her age."

Max looked at me grumpily. "Can't you do it?"

I shook my head. "Sorry buddy, you have been chosen."

Max put his head in his hand as the bathroom door finally opened and the girls pranced out. Allison was in a lacy white dress, cut high in the neck like mine, but also cut rather short at the leg. Her shapely legs looked about ten miles long, especially with the expensive looking, black stiletto ankle boots she was wearing. A thick black belt around her waist completed the look.

Lela was in basic black again, but whereas her dress from earlier had been simple, the one she was wearing now was bedecked with lace and sparkle. The entire top from armpits up was made of sheer lace. It looked uncomfortable as hell, and I was suddenly very glad for my dress. Lela's black heels weren't as high as mine or Allison's, but then again she didn't need any help making her legs look long anyhow.

Lucy was in crimson, and it made her olive skin stand out in stunning contrast. Her dress was simple, but fit her perfectly to accentuate her petite frame. Her shoes looked like the twin of Lela's.

I gestured towards the door. "Let's go get this over with."

We all left the room and made our way towards the stairs. Allison led the way like she owned the place, of course.

As soon as she was far enough ahead, Jason shuffled up beside me. "Why is Allison even coming?" he whispered.

"We made a deal," I answered simply.

"But it's probably not a good idea to let her meet werewolves that could potentially turn her," he went on.

"Just like it probably wasn't a good idea to keep me in the dark about Allison wanting someone to change her in the first place."

"I thought I had talked her out of it," he countered.

I shook my head. "If there's one important thing to learn about Allison, it's that you can never talk her out of anything."

Chase walked up on my other side to join our conversation. "Sounds like somebody else I know."

Jason chuckled. He looked my outfit up and down. "At least she can be talked *in* to stuff."

Chase laughed in return. Oh man, they were banding together against me. Now I'd never get anything accomplished, and with the heels I couldn't even run away.

Instead of running, I walked as fast as I could to catch up with the rest of our group. Chase and Jason fell behind, making wisecracks that I chose not to hear.

Max and Allison walked as far away from each other as possible without actually leaving the group. I joined arms with Lucy and walked a little farther ahead. I *so* didn't need to deal with their drama on top of everything else. We exited the front door and continued walking. The dance was being held, wait for it . . . in the woods. Big surprise there.

"I can't believe you actually want to go to this thing," I mentioned to Lucy conversationally.

"Yeah, well it could be fun," she answered, not meeting my eyes.

"Please, someone explain to me how this is supposed to be fun," I said sarcastically.

"Dancing can be fun Xoe. It might be nice to dance with . . . people," Lucy replied hesitantly.

Aha, the truth comes out. "And which people, pray tell, might be fun to dance with?" I prodded.

Lucy looked behind us to see how far back the others had fallen. We had a good bit of distance between us.

"Wait," I began, then asked, "Max?"

Lucy sighed. "No, not Max."

"Well I know it's not Jason," I prompted.

Lucy looked down at the ground. "It's Chase," she mumbled.

Wait, Lucy liked Chase? I definitely had not expected this. I mean, I shouldn't care really, but I did. I hated that I did. I loved Jason. I knew for a fact that he loved me back. I shouldn't give a damn who Chase dated. Damn . . . I totally cared.

I stumbled at her words, and in four-inch heels it was quite a stumble. Luckily since my arm was linked in Lucy's, I managed not to fall. "So . . . you like Chase?" I asked, looking for verification.

Lucy gave me a sharp look. "Not so loud Xoe!" she hissed.

"Okay," I soothed, "sorry. How long have you liked him?"

Lucy shrugged as a blush crept up her neck to her face. "I dunno," she mumbled. "For a while I guess. Do you think it's a bad idea?"

Did I think it was a bad idea? So many different ways to answer her question flooded through my mind, but none of them seemed good enough. None of them seemed honest either.

"Uh, do you think he likes you?" I asked in return, completely at a loss.

Lucy eyed me suspiciously. "Why are you getting all weird about this? Did he say something to you?"

"No," I answered quickly. "You just caught me off guard. I didn't realize he was your type."

"Since when do I have a type?" she asked.

I nodded and smiled. "Good point. I guess what I meant was," I began, "well, I don't really know what I meant. You just caught me off guard."

"So do you think it's a bad idea?" she prompted again.

I swallowed a lump in my throat. "No, I think it's a great idea."

Lucy smiled. I felt queasy. Sometimes the right answer isn't always the honest one.

# Chapter Eight

Jason walked up and put his arm around me. "What's wrong?" he whispered. "You look all flushed."

"Just feeling overheated again," I mumbled, waving my hand in front of my face to emphasize my point.

Lucy fell back to join the rest of the group as Jason gave my shoulders a reassuring squeeze, then led me on towards the meeting place. I had an urge to look behind us and see how close Chase and Lucy were walking. Don't worry, I resisted. I looked down at the ground instead, feeling like a terrible person.

In the time it had taken us to get ready, the barren meeting place had been completely transformed. Silken tents hung from the trees and glowed with the light of strategically placed candles. Some sort of hard surface had been lain for the dance floor. The wolves were dressed in gowns and tuxedos. Those who danced swayed to softly played, classical music. It all looked like something out of a fairytale. You had to hand it to them, werewolves sure knew how to throw a party.

By the time we arrived, the last slivers of sunlight had long since disappeared behind the mountains. The lack of sunlight left the dance area almost too dark. Then again, werewolves have some pretty impressive night vision, so they probably didn't worry too much about sufficient lighting.

Tensions seemed to have eased since the earlier meeting. Nobody paid us much mind. Lela and Allison were almost instantly snatched up as dance partners. Only moments later Lucy and Chase were snatched up as well . . . luckily not by each other.

I mentally slapped myself on the wrist for my thoughts as Jason twirled me out onto the dance floor. I had to catch myself against his chest to keep from falling. I laughed, "Remember the heels."

"I will not let you fall," he assured with a smile.

I tried to move and sway as effortlessly as those surrounding me, but I've just never been a good dancer. I've got decent coordination . . . decent enough to play sports at least, but the rhythm of dancing is simply beyond me. Jason didn't seem to mind as he gently spun me about, probably just enjoying the fact that I hadn't argued about dancing with him in the first place.

As the music slowed, he drew me in close. "You seem very tense tonight," he observed.

I took a deep breath and tried to release a bit of the tension. "It's been a long day," I explained.

He leaned down and kissed me softly, as if I might break. I didn't like the imagery of me being delicate, so I kissed him back fiercely. For a brief wonderful moment, everyone around us disappeared and it was just us two.

Our kiss was interrupted by someone tapping on Jason's shoulder. I opened my eyes to see Devin waiting patiently for our attention. He was dressed in all black again, just a slightly fancier version of all black.

Devin dipped his head in acknowledgment of my presence, then turned to Jason. "May I cut in?" he intoned.

He seriously chose that moment to interrupt us? He couldn't have waited a few more seconds? I looked at Jason and thought say no, say no, say no over and over again.

Jason gave me an apologetic smile. "Why of course," he answered.

Damn. Devin held out his hand to me and I reluctantly took it. His hands were rougher than I expected. I hadn't really pegged Devin as the hard labor type, but his hands bespoke a past, or maybe even a present, of hard work without gloves. I couldn't really picture Devin building furniture or installing tile. Maybe he gardened.

Devin led me away from Jason. He kept my hand in his, then placed his other hand lightly at my waist. He stood closer to me than I would have liked, but the dancing would have been awkward if he stood any farther. In the heels I was an inch or two taller than him.

"You've made quite an impression on our little community," he explained as we swayed slowly on the dance floor.

"Not on purpose," I mumbled. I tried to ignore the discomfort I felt at his hand at my waist. Yet another reason to not like dances. Too many people had an excuse to touch you.

I searched the crowd for someone to save me. Jason had disappeared. My eyes came across Chase, who was dancing with a petite, red-headed werewolf. He met my gaze and held it until Devin spun me in a different direction.

I couldn't find anyone else I

knew, so I figured I may as well make some conversation. "So . . . " I began, "which pack is yours?"

"I don't have one," Devin answered with an almost proud smile.

"Aren't werewolves, like, vulnerable without a pack?" I asked.

Devin shrugged. "If you find a pack for me to lead, let me know."

I furrowed my brow. "Why would you be the one to lead it?"

Devin swung me out and into a spin under our joined hands. He had to catch me behind my back before I fell. He chuckled at my clumsiness and held me a little too tightly.

"Do that again," I warned, "and you'll end up with third degree burns."

"Sorry," he conceded, but didn't loosen his grip. "No more spins. To answer your question, I'm too strong for any Alpha to let me into their pack for fear of a challenge. I'd have to form my own. I'm fine working with Abel for now. I've got diplomatic immunity."

I laughed. "And you were betting on me? Isn't it against the rules for politicians to take bets on the outcome of upcoming votes?"

Devin shrugged. "I never claimed to be a good politician. Actually, I'm really a rather terrible politician."

71

"Well you've got the charm down," I replied, "for those who can't see through it."

"And here I thought I had you fooled," Devin joked. "I'm more off my game than I thought."

After a moment of just dancing, he spoke again. "I'm actually surprised you came to this tonight. It's not a mandatory event."

I glared at him. I've been told I have a pretty good glare, but he just kept on smiling.

"The girls wanted to come," I explained. "Don't ask me why."

"Well you look lovely," he replied. "I like you with your hair up."

I glared even harder. "If you're trying to flirt with me, you should know that you're howling up the wrong tree."

Devin laughed. "Sorry, it's in my nature, the charm and all. I don't mean anything by it."

I scowled, but said nothing. I had a feeling that Devin meant something by every little thing he did.

"My you are quite a tough nut to crack," he continued casually. "Most people really do find me charming."

I smiled sweetly back at him.

"Most people are also morons."

"Well put," he replied. "Though you are a demon attempting to form a werewolf pack. Some might question your intelligence."

I raised my eyebrows at him, surprised he had finally said something insulting. "Good thing I'm not here to prove my intelligence."

He laughed. "Nope, you're here to prove your brawn. I think you'd probably have a better time with intelligence."

I smirked at him. "You'd be surprised."

Devin laughed again. "I've no doubt about that."

The music changed tempo again. Two songs was enough. I could probably escape now. I pulled away.

"I have got to go find my boyfriend," I announced, just to once again verify that Devin wasn't getting any funny ideas.

I didn't think he was, but you couldn't be too cautious with such things. He pulled back and kissed my hand and I let him. He could make out with the back of my palm all he wanted, if it meant I didn't have to dance with him anymore.

I pulled my hand away and wove my way through dancing couples in search of Jason. Who I found was Chase. He was sitting on a small bench next to Lela with a plate of food in his lap.

I hurried over to sit on the bench beside him before someone else could pull me into a dance. We sat in silence for a few minutes. Another handsome werewolf came and pulled Lela back out onto the floor. She went willingly. I looked down at Chase's untouched food.

"Why aren't you eating," I questioned.

Chase shrugged. "I'm not hungry, but the plate of food seems to be a deterrent for any girls hoping to make me dance more." He nodded his head off to our left.

Four women were standing there watching him, waiting for him to finish eating. Now that was just plain creepy. I'd never been to an actual dance, but I sincerely hoped that the people I went to school with weren't nearly as . . . predatory as the werewolves seemed to be.

Some random guy in a dark gray suit came striding towards us. "Crap," I muttered. "Give me your plate."

"No way," Chase argued. "They'll pounce as soon as I put it down."

The guy was getting closer. I grabbed the corner of Chase's plate and tried to tug it away from him. He tugged back. "I don't think so," he whispered. "I've already been groped by three different women. You've only danced with one guy so far."

I tugged harder. "Yeah, but it was a super long dance."

Chase tugged back. The paper plate ripped and sent food flying to land right by the feet of the guy now standing in front of us.

"Would you like to-" the guy began.

I handed the guy my half of the paper plate. "Sorry, just got asked," I mumbled.

Chase chucked his plate half into a nearby trashcan as I dragged him out onto the dance floor. He wrapped his arms around me hesitantly. "I thought the idea was to not have to dance."

"Better with you than with some random guy," I grumbled.

Chase smiled. "Well maybe I'd rather dance with some random girl."

"Well then maybe you should have just given me your plate," I retorted.

He sighed loudly. "As long as you don't try and grope me, I guess I can deal with it."

I laughed, glad Devin hadn't tried to grope me.

"These shoes make you really tall," Chase remarked.

"And really unstable," I added. "So please, no dramatic spins."

He tsk'ed at me. "There you go, ruining

all of my fun."

I noticed Lucy dancing with Max, while she gave me a confused and slightly hurt look. Great, now Lucy was going to be mad at me for stealing her dance. I really had no choice . . . honest. I glanced past Lucy and Max to see a little girl with long brown hair giving Lucy the same look that Lucy had given me.

This was all just too uncomfortable. I looked around for Jason, to see if I could maybe give some girl dancing with him a hurt and confused look, but he was still nowhere to be found.

"I'm sorry again about earlier," Chase added, drawing my attention back to him.

I bit my lower lip. "It's okay," I mumbled in reply. "I overreacted. I've been a bit . . . tense lately."

See? Who says I can't be diplomatic?

Chase lifted my chin up so I'd meet his eyes. It was weird being at almost exactly eye-level with him. The somewhat intimate gesture made my pulse speed up.

"I'm not here for your dad," Chase stated. "Not anymore. We don't need to discuss it any further than that. I just want you to know. I'm here because I want to look out for you, not because I have to."

Oh geez. What the heck was I supposed

to say to that? I looked back down. "Um . . . thanks."

He nodded, as if an 'um thanks' was a sufficient response to what he had said. I had a feeling in my stomach like I either needed to throw up, pass out, or scream. Things were getting way too complicated.

"I wish we were home," I whispered.

"Me too," Chase replied. He was silent for a moment, then went on. "So, speaking of home, what's going to happen when we get there?"

I pulled back a little so I could meet his eyes. "What do you mean?"

Chase shrugged. "Since the time I first met you we've been dealing with one issue or another. This is the last issue. If everything works out, what will we do when we get back home?"

"Well," I began, not knowing what to say. "I still have school . . ."

Chase nodded but didn't reply and I started to feel like a total ass. He was asking if I wanted him to stay in town. I should have told him to do whatever he wanted. I should have told him to go and find a nice demon girl to date.

"I'll still need help with my lessons," I began, "so, you know . . . you should stick around."

Chase nodded and held me a little tighter. I didn't protest. Bad Xoe. Very, very bad Xoe.

"Plus, your mom would be totally bummed if I left," Chase joked, trying to lighten the mood.

I laughed so abruptly that I almost choked. "I will *never* understand why she likes you so much. I wouldn't be surprised if when we got back she invited you to live with us."

Chase smiled. "Well, I wouldn't put it past her, but I think my connection to your dad might stop her."

I nodded. "Which is why I'm surprised she likes you in the first place. She wants absolutely nothing to do with my dad. Anytime I mention him she clams up and goes all pale, so I've just stopped  trying. It would be nice to be able to have my lessons at home, but I guess I understand where she's coming from too."

"Well she did see him kill a guy," Chase added.

"Well yeah," I argued, "but it was in defense of us. The guy pushed my baby stroller over apparently."

"Well look at you," Chase taunted, "actually *defending* your father."

"Only on that one little act," I sulked. "I

78

have *not* forgotten my abandonment."

Chase looked at me seriously. "He talked about you a lot, before you actually met."

I gave him a questioning look. "What would he have to talk about? He didn't even know me."

"He checked in on you," he replied. "even though you didn't know it."

"And how do you even know this?" I asked, feeling flustered.

Chase flushed a little at that. "Well, I went along a few times . . . when he checked on you."

"You what!" I exclaimed, eliciting a few questioning stares from the nearest dancers. I lowered my voice, "You *spied* on me?"

"No," Chase said calmly. "I *checked* on you, along with your father. Sometimes when he couldn't make it, he'd send me to check on you by myself."

"Um," I began nervously, "How long ago did you start *checking* on me."

The thought of Chase seeing me as a nerdy, gangly preteen gave me shivers. The thought of him knowing I used to wear high-waters everyday, because I could never find jeans long enough for me was even worse.

Chase smiled. "Only in the past two years."

Oh thank the gods . . . but still, it rankled that Chase had *known* me in a sense for the past two years, when I only first met him around a month ago.

"Well, I just don't like this at all," I decided out loud.

Chase chuckled. "Don't worry, I won't tell anyone you went through a Shakira faze."

Well damn.

# Chapter Nine

Before I realized it, several songs had passed. We didn't see any of our would-be escorts in sight, so Chase and I went looking for the rest of our group. We'd only been there maybe 30 minutes, but it was so past time to get back to our rooms. We'd made an appearance, and that was good enough dammit.

We managed to gather up Lucy and Max pretty quickly. Lela and Allison had to be pried from a group of men fawning over them. All that was left was Jason . . . and we couldn't find him. I went from being pissed that he'd abandoned me, to slightly worried.

After combing the entire gathering area, we started sweeping outwards into the woods. We split into pairs: Lucy with Allison, Chase with Lela, and me with Max. Each pair had one wolf to help scent Jason out.

After only about a minute I got tired of

Max having to catch me, so I took off the heels in favor of walking barefoot. There was only a sliver of moon in the sky (a werewolf gathering near the full moon would have been disastrous). I just hoped that I wouldn't find any snakes or spiders with my bare feet.

Several more minutes of stumbling through the underbrush, and we finally heard voices. Well, Max heard voices, and made a shushing motion at me as we crept forward, then I finally heard them. There were four figures in a clearing ahead of us. One looked like Jason, but in the dark I couldn't be sure. I looked at Max for verification and he nodded.

I leaned against a nearby tree so I could go on tip-toes and try and get a better look. As my hands pushed against the rough bark, the tree made a loud cracking sound. I cringed and turned my attention back to the clearing.

All four figures had whipped around to stare in the direction of the noise. Without a word spoken, the Jason-looking figure strode in our direction, leaving the other three to stand and stare.

When what was indeed Jason reached us, he grabbed my shoulders and steered me back towards the dance, leaving Max to follow. I stubbed my toe on a tree root as he hurried me along. He caught me before I went down, but I was still pissed.

"What the heck is going on?" I spat, trying to ignore the pain in my toe.

"Why aren't you wearing shoes?" Jason asked, ignoring my question.

"Oh, I dunno," I said sarcastically. "It was a little difficult to go wandering through the woods in four-inch heels, in search of my boyfriend who abandoned me all night."

Jason bit his tongue before he could say something to further piss me off. Max stayed out of it. Very wise of him.

Without another word, Jason gathered me up in his arms and started carrying me purposefully back towards the gathering. I was too confused to fight much, so I just wrapped my arms around his neck and waited. I'd tear him a new one once we were back in our rooms.

We got close to the gathering, and what I hoped would be where I could walk for myself again. No such luck. Jason skirted around the clearing, avoiding any onlookers.

"Max," Jason ordered. "Get the others."

Max left us without another word.

I'd had enough. I went through the visualization my dad had taught me. Soon enough I was being dropped to my feet as Jason raised a hand to his burned neck. It was only a mild burn, like a bad sunburn, but the initial shock was enough to get Jason to put me down.

"You need to explain what's going on," I said calmly with my feet firmly planted on the ground, then added, "Right now."

Jason stared at me in consternation, his lips in a tight, unrelenting line. "I didn't know there would be other vampires here," he replied.

Other vampires? A million thoughts raced through my head. I knew quite a bit about vampires, seeing as I was dating one. Yet, Jason wasn't scary to me, he was just . . . Jason. Other vampires were scary. The were also rare.

Few victims survived the transition to become vampires. Those that did tended to be loners, or stayed with relatively small groups. I had assumed I'd go my whole life without bumping into another one, or at least not so soon.

"What?" I questioned.

"Other vampires," he affirmed. "Several of the packs hired them. Apparently they're afraid of you and your father . . . mainly your father. They wanted back up just in case."

Now I was really confused. How were people supposed to be scared of me when I'd just give them sunburns . . . or set their cars on fire, or maybe burn them to death. Ok, I was moderately scary. Now my dad I understood, he is much more than moderately scary.

"But, he's not here," I argued.

"They're being cautious," he explained, wiping his palm nervously across his face. Jason had to be pretty worked up for his nervous ticks to show this much. "After Dan, and then Nick . . . werewolves tend to gossip. Stories get embellished."

"So why hire vampires?" I asked.

"Since vampires don't have much affiliation group-wise, they often tend to work as mercenaries of a sort," he answered.

I shrugged. "Okay, that still doesn't explain why you ditched me all night to have a mysterious meeting in a clearing with a gang of vampire mercenaries."

"I know two of the other vampires that were hired," he admitted with a shrug. "I needed to make sure that they meant you no harm. Most vampires aren't like me. They would kill you simply to see what your blood tasted like. Rarely do you find a demon of any magnitude vulnerable. Chase may be in danger of being attacked as well."

"So basically, more monster-types out for my blood?" I asked.

Supernaturals really did have a weird obsession with blood. Vampires needed it, werewolves reacted to it, bad people tried to steal it for nefarious purposes. Not for the first

85

time I found myself glad that the only blood I needed or wanted was the stuff running through my veins.

Jason nodded. "We shouldn't have come here. We need to be careful."

I sighed. "Like that's anything new. I'm almost constantly with a vampire, another demon, and three werewolves. I wouldn't say I'm exactly vulnerable."

Jason grabbed my shoulders to emphasize his point. "Some of them are stronger than me. I can't protect you."

"Oh yeah?" I said, eyebrow raised. "I'm not worried until I find out they're stronger than *me*."

I turned around and sauntered away. That's right ladies and gentlemen, Xoe Meyers can saunter. Stick that in your pipe and smoke it.

# Chapter Ten

I woke up beside Jason. I was still slightly peeved, but he had apologized once we got back to the room, and I had been in serious need of some snuggling. He really was just looking out for my best interest, even though he was doing it in an overbearing way.

I had done my best not to think about Chase lying silently on his cot. I would have given a large sum of money to know what he was thinking. Then again, maybe it was best that I didn't know. He was my friend and I refused to let things get awkward.

Sensing that I was awake, Jason snuggled me closer. Jason doesn't sleep, so when we stay the night together, he usually just lies next to me waiting for me to wake. Sounds boring to me, but he doesn't seem to mind.

I turned over to glance at the clock. 6:30am. Ick. I had a breakfast meeting to go to at 8:00. I was the only one of our group allowed at the meeting. I had to present my proposal to form our pack. Lela had helped me write it, but I was still worried. Public speaking is not my forte.

I gave Jason a smile, then rolled out of bed and stumbled toward the bathroom to take a shower. Chase seemed to be asleep, and Max was just a lump under his blankets. Before I could pass through the doorway, Jason was just suddenly there in front of me. He pulled me in and tried to kiss me.

"Hey man," I argued in a whisper, pushing against his chest. "Morning breath."

Jason shrugged. "Don't care,"

I shrugged in return, and pulled his face down to my level. The kiss started out soft, then intensified, making me forget all about my morning breath. I leaned against Jason's chest to assure that my footing remained stable.

Jason took this as a sign to kiss me further, his hands tightly gripping the sides of my waist. With all of the stress in our lives, we had kind of let our relationship fall to the sidelines. I realized that Jason had been so intent on being my bodyguard, that he had forgotten to be my boyfriend. I'd been so intent on trying to take care of everyone, that I hadn't been paying him much attention either.

We heard a throat clear somewhere beside us. Jason and I both pulled away from the kiss to regard the interruption. Chase was standing in front of us looking grumpy and half-asleep. There was no way Jason hadn't heard him walking up. I glared up at Jason.

"Um," Chase mumbled. "I need to use the bathroom."

My face flared with heat that had nothing to do with my demon powers. I tried to flee the bathroom doorway as quickly as possible to hide my blush. Jason laughed as he followed me out into the main room.

Max was awake and perched on his bed, because I totally needed someone else to observe my embarrassment. "Are you overheating again or something?" he questioned.

Jason walked up to hug me from behind. Max glanced at the bathroom where Chase was, then back to us. His mouth formed into an "O" of understanding. I blushed even harder as I hurried to the adjoining room door. I would be showering in the girls' room today.

All of the girls were still soundly asleep. I would have been soundly asleep too if I had any other choice. I crept past their beds and into the bathroom, shutting the door gently behind me.

I undressed and hopped into the shower. I turned on the water, standing clear so as not to get hit by the initial cold water, but my efforts were in vain. Someone had left the shower nozzle pointing outwards, and since I hadn't closed the curtain yet, water sprayed all over the bathroom. It completely soaked my pajamas as well as the small towel that was placed on the floor. Gre-eat.

I adjusted the shower head and closed the curtain. I'd clean up the mess later. Finding that someone had left their travel bottles of shampoo and conditioner in there, I helped myself. I hate those little hotel two-in-one shampoo/conditioners, and I wasn't really in a mood to be polite.

The shampoo smelled strongly of some herb, maybe rosemary. My guess was that the shampoo belonged to Lela. It seemed like her kind of scent. I absorbed myself into the smell, trying to relax a little. I had just promised myself that I wouldn't let things get awkward with Chase, and here I was, hiding in the shower, feeling embarrassed and awkward. Stupid boys. I was actually kind of glad that I got to go to this morning's meeting by myself.

When I finally stepped out of the shower and dried myself off with one of the white towels that the inn supplied, I realized that I'd forgotten to grab a change of clothes, and my pajamas were thoroughly soaked. Damn.

I wrapped my towel around me as tightly as possible and went out into the bedroom. I sat down by a sleeping Lucy and attempted to shake her awake. She mumbled something unintelligible at me, then rolled over, burrito-ing herself up in her blankets.

I tried Allison next. She actually half woke up. "What d'you want?" she mumbled.

"I left my suitcase in the other room," I whispered back.

Allison frowned at me as she woke up a bit more. "So go get it loser."

I stood, showing her that I was just in a towel.

"Stop being a baby," she grumbled before burying her face back in her pillow. Double damn.

I readjusted my towel and made my way back to the boys' room, hoping they had all gone to breakfast. Sadly, only either Max or Jason had gone. I didn't know which since one of them was in the closed bathroom with the shower running. A freshly showered, and thankfully dressed Chase was sitting on his cot putting his shoes on.

Feeling like I was in a really cheesy romantic comedy, I silently walked over to my suitcase that I'd left between the room's two beds. I was ignoring Chase so hard, that I didn't realize he'd gotten up to walk towards the door. I turned around with my clothes clutched against my chest, and almost ran straight into him.

We both stared at each other for a moment. He tugged at the bottom edge of his shirt like it needed to be adjusted. "Um, sorry about earlier-" he began.

"No problem," I interrupted before he could say something to make me feel even more embarrassed.

I clutched my towel tightly and looked down at the floor, not wanting to discuss it further.

He just stood there, at a loss for words. Dark, slightly wavy hair slicked back with moisture, looking scrumptious. Oh geez.

I brushed past him as quickly as possible and bolted back into the girls' room. Not awkward at all, and my name is Queen Elizabeth Mary.

# Chapter Eleven

After I got dressed I marched back into the boys' room, head held high. I was all ready to be smooth and not at all awkward.

"Why are you walking like that?" Max asked as soon as I entered the room.

I kept my nose up just as high as ever. "I have no idea what you're talking about. I'm off to my meeting."

I lowered my nose enough to see Chase staring at me. As soon as I noticed him, he quickly looked down at his hands sitting in his lap. I looked away just as quickly. Totally not awkward.

"I'll walk you down," Jason offered, turning my attention to him.

"You can't come in with me, remember?"

Jason smiled. "I'll wait for you outside the door."

The appearance of the other vampires had made my already paranoid boyfriend even more so. I made myself smile and told myself that paranoia couldn't hurt, and it was probably warranted anyhow. Heck, maybe he wasn't paranoid at all, maybe he was just smarter than the rest of us.

I nodded and held out my hand to him. We left the room without another glance, but I could feel eyes on me as I left. It was probably Max, wondering why I was once again acting like a crazy person. You'd think he'd be used to it by now.

Fortunately today's meeting was labeled as casual, so I'd dressed down in faded jeans, dark green v-neck t-shirt, and my trusty sneakers. I felt much more comfortable in my casual wear. Hard as I tried, dressing up made me feel embarrassed and weird. Plus, I like to be in shoes I can run away in. One should always be prepared to run away.

The meeting was being held in one of the small conference rooms that the inn boasted, down by the lobby. I left Jason outside the door with a quick kiss, then went in without knocking.

I was early (a rarity for me), and only a few of the seats were filled. I sat down at the small rectangular table in the small rectangular room. Across the table from me sat bear-man (who introduced himself as Mike) and a dark skinned woman that I guessed would be about 6'3" when she stood. Deep brown, dense curls foamed around her face. She introduced herself as Darla.

Though Darla and Mike sat next to one-another, I sensed some major animosity going on. They each spoke to me, but had looks of utter distaste on their faces when they were not the one speaking.

"So you're the demon," Darla said to me conversationally, voice only expressing mild interest.

"Yep," I shrugged. "That's me."

"You know you better watch your back around here," she stated, absolutely no emotion in her voice.

"Is that a threat?" I asked casually.

She shrugged. "Not really. Just a fact."

How could something 'not really' be a threat? I turned my attention from Darla as the rest of our group began to file into the room. Everyone avoided the seats directly next to me until Devin entered, sitting next to me and even scooting a little closer.

His vested interest in me had me even more worried than Darla's non-threat. I glanced down at his arm on the table, *way* too close to mine, and scooted my arm a few more inches away. Devin didn't seem to notice. He was in all black again. He either needed a serious wardrobe makeover, or he was constantly monochrome for a reason. A sign of neutrality maybe? Though, for someone who was supposed to be neutral, he didn't resemble Switzerland in the slightest.

Abel entered last and stood at the head of the table. Greta, my new favorite werewolf, was nowhere to be seen. I guess Mike didn't think she was needed. I was with Mike on this one.

No one spoke as Abel went to a coffee pot in the corner and poured himself a cup. I was told that this was a breakfast meeting, but they must have just meant that it occurred at breakfast time, because I didn't see any food in sight. My stomach growled at the thought, and Devin turned to raise an eyebrow at me. No one else seemed to notice, but I was in a room full of werewolves, so I knew they all heard it.

Abel placed his coffee on the table without taking a single sip. He was dressed down today in a tight gray t-shirt and expensive looking jeans. His hair was loose and flowed long and thick, nearly to his waist. Having hair that long would drive my crazy. Knowing me, I'd probably slam it in car doors and strangle myself in my sleep.

Abel cleared his throat. "Today's meeting," he began, "has been called so that one, Alexondra Meyers, may state her need for the formation of a new pack. Her statement will be heard in full, then you will have an opportunity to question her. After that, the meeting will adjourn, and we will place the matter to a vote tonight."

Apparently finished speaking, Abel sat and turned his gaze to me. His gaze was intense, like he was trying to prod me into action with the powers of his mind alone. When I didn't do anything except sit there and look nervous, he motioned with his hand for me to rise.

I stood hesitantly and cleared my throat. Please don't mess up, please don't mess up. "Um hi," I said, giving a feeble wave to the room. 'Um hi'? Great way to start Xoe. Werewolves responded to confidence and aggression, not meek nervousness.

I took a deep breath to gather my composure, and went on, "I'm here today to petition to form a pack-"

"Tell us something we don't know," a younger woman with hair and skin as pale as mine mumbled. I hadn't noticed her at the meeting the day before, but then again I had been a little too busy worrying about my own presentation to pay much attention to anyone else's.

At a simultaneous dirty look from me, Devin, and Abel, she promptly shut up. Darla covered her mouth with her hand to hide her silent laughter. It didn't help much, her amber eyes were shiny with amusement. At least someone was having a good time.

I stood a little straighter and tried to remember what Lela had told me to say. "The only wolves in my area have unanimously agreed to be part of my pack. My bid as Alpha has been approved by the coalition leader. Members of my soon-to-be pack stood witness to the event that qualified me as such."

"Murder doesn't make you Alpha," Mike interjected.

"But self-defense after a personal challenge does," Devin countered.

Mike opened his mouth to say more, but Abel interrupted him. "Questions and opinions will be held until after Alexondra's proposal."

I took a deep breath and went on. "I will live by werewolf law, though I am not a werewolf, and I will protect my pack with my life." The end, I thought to myself . . . hopefully it wasn't my end.

I sat without another word. There was a brief moment of silence, then everyone erupted into a mixture of excited and angry chatter. Darla just sat back and smiled. Either she cared little enough about what was happening to find it funny, or she knew something I didn't. I was betting on the latter.

Once Abel calmed the crowd, the questioning began, and oh, what a questioning it was. They basically just repeated that I wasn't a werewolf, that I was a murderer, and so on and so forth.

When the meeting finally ended, I let everyone leave before me. No need to get accosted in the hallway if I could help it.

"You did good," Devin observed, still sitting beside me.

"You don't stand a chance," Abel added, head in his hands.

We were the only three left in the room.

"We could just push it through without a vote," Devin suggested.

Abel shook his head. "It would be chaos."

"Not that I mind," I interrupted. "But why do you guys care?"

Abel stared at me for a long time, before finally speaking. "Our packs are vulnerable," he explained. "Our most recent incident has shown us that." The incident he was referring to was the killing of several werewolves by the same group that kidnapped and tried to kill me.

"If you are bound by werewolf law," he explained, "it will give demons and other supernaturals pause before messing with any of our wolves. Everyone is made more wary where demons are involved. Demons live forever. That's a long time to run away from vengeance."

"But I'm only a half-demon," I countered. "I killed Dan by accident, and had to be rescued from my kidnappers by my dad. I'm going to have a normal human lifespan. No one is going to be scared of my vengeance."

"But very few know any of that," Devin explained. "The human lifespan maybe, but that's it. It's the same principle that someone would use in burglarizing a home. One home has a big angry dog, one home does not. Which would you choose to rob?"

I was beginning to understand where they were coming from. We didn't have to be that scary, just scarier than the next group. "So, I'm your big angry dog?"

Abel nodded and smiled his perfect smile. "Exactly."

I stood and shook my head. "I hope you two know what you're doing."

Abel turned to Devin. "Might I have a moment alone with Alexondra?"

Devin nodded and offered me his hand.

I looked at the hand suspiciously. "If you kiss my hand again I'm going to smack you."

Devin smiled. "A simple handshake then?"

I smiled back and offered my hand. He shook it, a nice, proper handshake, then quickly left the room like a good little lackey.

As soon as the door shut I turned to face Abel.

He looked down then up at me again, nervous. Suspicious.

"As coalition leader, I would like to offer you my protection Alexondra."

The wording made me laugh. Well maybe not the wording, but the phrase itself. It just seemed like something someone would say in a bad mobster flick.

I stifled myself mid-laugh. "Um, that's nice and all, but why?"

Abel looked down at the table. "We're asking a lot of you."

I still wasn't getting it. "I thought protection was the whole point of giving me a pack. You pretty much offered me your protection with that offer."

Abel shook his head. "Not my personal protection. Under pack law, if someone kills you, we'll hunt them down and kill them. We have enforcers for that. What I'm offering you is different. If anyone challenges your dominance, they will in effect be challenging mine."

I snorted. "You're going to have a lot of challenges to your dominance then."

Abel wasn't smiling at all now. "Not as many as you might think. The only ones who challenge you are stupid. My protection will hold the stupid ones at bay. They've learned to be scared of me. They don't have enough experience to be scared of you, yet."

I shook my head. "I think you have the wrong impression of me. I'm really not that scary."

"How much do you know of your heritage?" he asked abruptly.

The sudden subject change threw me off. "My heritage?" I stammered.

"Demons have quite the history," he explained. "If more knew about that history, you would never have had a single challenger to begin with."

Now I was even more confused. Demons were relatively unknown, even in the supernatural community. Few knew what we could do, especially since our powers varied so greatly. It made us wild cards. Some of the cards would only give you a paper cut, and others would mush you to a pulp. It was an intimidating concept, but it wasn't exactly a history.

My stomach growled again.

Abel took a deep breath. "I'm getting off topic. The point is, I'm offering you my protection. Do you accept?"

"Oh no you don't," I replied. "What's this history you're talking about."

He smiled. "Have your father explain it to you sometime. Do you accept?"

I squinted at him suspiciously. "What does accepting entail?"

"Nothing," he replied, "except that you acknowledge my dominance, and my right to protect you."

I did *not* like the sound of that. "Your *right*? That sounds like I'd be your property."

Abel shrugged. "Only as far as public perception is concerned. You would not in truth be mine. Usually protection is only offered to a spouse or a child."

I blinked slowly, completely taken aback and not sure what to think. I was pretty sure he wasn't asking me to be his spouse, because ew, but there was the possibility that he was asking me to pretend to be his spouse.

"I don't think so," I replied sharply.

Abel just sat silently for a moment and regarded me. "It would help protect your friends . . . " he began.

I cocked my head in question. "In what way?"

Abel smiled. He knew he had me as soon as he mentioned my friends, damn it. "If you're mine, and they're yours, to mess with one would be to mess with all."

"So I pretend to be *yours*, and we'll stop getting picked on?" I asked.

Abel smiled again, the smug bastard. "Yes."

"Fine." I stood.

Abel stood and put his hand on the back of my chair to bar my way. "So you agree?"

I glared up at him. "I said *fine*, didn't I?"

Abel grinned from ear to ear. "We'll make the announcement tonight."

With that, I left the room to meet Jason in the hallway, leaving Abel alone to grin over his victory. I had a feeling there was more to this protection ownership than Abel was saying. All I had agreed to was being *his* in name only, but the thought still rankled. A demon's pride and all of that.

"How'd it go?" Jason asked anxiously as soon as he saw me. The fact that he had to ask at all meant someone had prevented him from standing anywhere near the door.

I kept walking and he fell into stride beside me. I shrugged. "I'm a big angry dog, and everyone wants to rob us, and I belong to an egocentric werewolf."

"Am I supposed to know what that means?" he asked.

"No," I answered and kept walking.

"What do you mean *belong*?" he asked trailing behind me.

"I'm not really sure," I replied morosely.

Jason grabbed my arm. He looked pissed. "What do you mean *belong,* Xoe?"

I shrugged, suddenly embarrassed. "It would be for the public eye only. If everyone else thinks I belong to him, they're going to back off."

I could feel tears welling behind my eyes and I didn't know why. I'm not much of a crier, but I had a feeling that I was overwhelmed just enough for it to happen.

"Ok," he responded, like he was trying to calm a spooked horse. "Then explain the big angry dog."

I couldn't bring myself to answer. The tears started to spill over. I'd been compared to a female dog a time or two, but never to a guard dog. Just call me Cujo.

# Chapter Twelve

Instead of going straight back to the room, Jason accompanied me to the lobby for the complimentary breakfast, which was luckily still going on. I didn't really feel hungry anymore, but I needed a distraction, so I busied myself with the nifty waffle maker that was set out on the counter, while Jason snagged us a table.

Plate piled high with food and coffee in hand, I sat down across from Jason, who sat with only a cup of coffee. I raised an eyebrow at him.

"I ate earlier," he explained.

Okay, I had to ask. "Um . . . what about your other hunger?"

Jason cleared his throat uncomfortably. "I took care of that earlier as well."

I wasn't sure when he would have had the chance, probably in the early morning hours while I was still asleep. I briefly wondered if he had been out hunting with werewolves . . . or other vampires, but I didn't question him further.

Thinking of Jason sucking the blood from Thumper or Bambi gave me the serious creeps, thinking of it as a group activity was just a little too much for me. I'd like to say it didn't give me occasional doubts, but it totally did. I tried to compare it to eating a hamburger, but it still didn't sit right.

Lucy, Allison, and Lela entered the lobby together. Lucy was the first to sit down, bagel and a cup of apple juice in hand. She took a sip of juice then turned to face me. "What on earth were you going on about this morning?" she asked.

Jason raised his eyebrows curiously.

"I forgot my clothes in the other room," I mumbled.

Lucy raised her hands in a 'so what?' gesture. "And? You had a towel."

"Geez, no one understands a little modesty these days," I replied sarcastically.

Lucy looked at me skeptically. "Since when are you modest?"

I was beginning to blush again. "I need more coffee," I stated. I jumped up and quickly hurried over to the coffee pot.

When I eventually returned to the table,

Allison and Lela had seated themselves as well. The table was a little cramped with five chairs, but I managed to wiggle my way back into my seat. No one else mentioned my morning escapades.

Jason caught my eye as I sipped my coffee. I smiled reassuringly at him. That seemed to be enough, as he rejoined the girls' discussion on what to do today. There were a few optional scheduled activities, but I for one had had quite enough of the other werewolves for the day.

Lucy, who had been leafing through a small local newspaper, turned her attention back to the table. "There's a local art fair going on," she announced. "We could go check it out."

I shrugged. "Sounds good to me." I turned to regard Jason. I already knew he would come, but it's always polite to ask.

Jason smiled. "If we must," he conceded.

"Oh," Lucy cut in, "How did the meeting go?"

Well there it was, I had managed to block it out of my head for a full five minutes. "We'll talk about it later," I mumbled.

Lucy stared at me for a heartbeat and must have seen something in my expression, because she changed the subject back to the art fair. "So we'll gather our stuff and go once we finish eating?"

I smiled in relief and nodded. "Yeah, we'll grab our stuff and see if Max or Chase want to come."

Lucy smiled a little bigger at the mention of Chase and I cringed. Really, I should be trying to set the two of them up. I *would* try and set them up. They were both my friends. If they could be happy together, then they should.

In the end, Allison, Lela, and Max opted for the werewolf agenda. So, it was just me, Lucy, Jason, and Chase that left the inn in the giant SUV. I got to drive, and Lucy instantly called shotgun, leaving the boys to sit in the back.

I could tell Lucy was hoping this would turn into a double date type of scenario as she sat in the passenger seat with a serene smile on her face. I strengthened my resolve to not be jealous, and just the fact that I had to do that made me feel incredibly guilty.

We pulled up to the large, grassy park where the art market was set up, but there wasn't a single empty parking space in the area. We drove in circles for a few minutes before giving up and parking on a residential street a few blocks away.

We got out of the SUV and started

walking with Chase in the lead, then me and Lucy, and Jason brought up the rear. I playfully shoved Lucy forward to walk next to Chase and fell back a few steps to walk with Jason. I twined my fingers around his, and for the first time that morning started to actually enjoy myself.

The art market was slightly more interesting than the clothes shopping Allison usually conned me into. The vendors ranged from traditional paintings and crafts, to natural products and vegan food. The food was donation only. If you could afford it, you added money to a jar on the counter, if not, you still got a plate. Everyone got to eat.

Chase wandered off to a booth filled with colorful metalworks, while I browsed some landscapes with Jason and Lucy. I gave Jason's hand a squeeze to get his attention. When he looked down I gestured that I was going to step away for a second and pulled my hand out of his. He looked skeptical as I went off in the direction Chase had gone, but smiled back when I smiled reassuringly at him with a wink.

I walked up to casually stand by Chase's side. "So," I began. "You're single, right?"

Chase turned his attention from a large metal scorpion to regard me. "Yes?" he replied like it was a question.

I nodded and looked down, feeling awkward. I fondled a small metal frog and considered getting it for my mom.

"You know, Lucy is single too," I went on.

Chase turned his gaze back to the table, but still asked, "So what's your point?"

"No point," I shrugged, heart racing. At that moment I was very glad that Chase was a demon and not a werewolf, and therefore probably couldn't hear my heart racing . . . probably.

"Let's join the others," Chase suggested, changing the subject awkwardly. "Jason looks bored already," he added.

I turned in the direction Chase was looking to see Jason pretending that he wasn't watching us. I walked back to Jason without another word with Chase following close behind me.

I put my hand back in Jason's when we reached him and he looked down at me in question. I shrugged and frowned in return. I'd explain it to him later.

Lucy and I took to browsing the booths as the boys took a seat at a picnic table to wait on us. Lucy was instantly drawn to a table supplying handcrafted herbal soaps and lotions. I followed her, more interested in just having some girl time than I was in the soaps.

As Lucy sniffed the random bricks, a small section of lavender scented goods caught my attention. I love lavender. They even had lavender scented shampoo and conditioner.

Since I hadn't brought any of my own, and didn't want to keep using up the mystery shampoo I'd used that morning, I went ahead and grabbed some. I handed the bottles and my money to the elderly woman manning the booth, and she packaged them up in a cute little paper bag with dried herbs attached to one of the handles.

Lucy didn't end up buying anything from the stand. She looked at my bag and I shrugged, then we headed towards the next booth that sported scarves and purses.

"So what were you and Chase talking about?" she questioned.

"You," I replied with a playful smile.

"You *didn't*," she squealed as she punched me in the arm.

I grabbed at the sudden throbbing pain in my arm and scowled at Lucy. Sometimes she forgets that she's a werewolf now, and her punches hurt a lot more than they used to.

Her hand fluttered up to her face in realization. "Sorry Xoe!" she exclaimed. "I'm still not used to being stronger."

I nodded and we started walking again.

"So what did he say when you talked to him?" she questioned nervously.

"Um," I began.

"Well this already doesn't sound good," she interrupted.

"Well," I began again, "he just seemed uncomfortable talking about it to me."

"Allison must be right then," Lucy replied sullenly.

I grabbed her arm to stop her mid-stride. "Wait. What?"

Lucy scrunched her eyebrows at me. "She said she already told you."

I shook my head. I had a feeling I already knew, but I asked anyway. "Told me what?"

Lucy looked at me like I was being stupid. "Chase is in love with you. I was skeptical at first, but now I'm pretty sure Al is right. She said she told you."

I shook my head. She had told me, but I had been nursing my wounds in a hot bath, half delirious from being held hostage and beaten and bruised. I hadn't taken the conversation seriously, as we'd all been through a lot, and Allison had just needed something else to focus on.

"He's not in love with me," I mumbled.

Lucy looked at me like I was a misbehaving child. "I know you've noticed Xoe, even if you don't wan't to admit it."

I shrugged and couldn't quite meet her eyes. "I know he cares about me, a little, but he's not in love with me."

"He looks at you the exact same way Jason looks at you," she replied bluntly.

"Well he needs to stop," I replied.

Lucy raised an eyebrow at me again. "So you don't feel anything for him, anything at all?"

I once again couldn't meet her eyes. "I don't know."

"Oh Xoe," Lucy consoled, annunciating her words slowly. "What are you going to do?"

I shrugged. "Nothing I guess. I'll just ignore it and hope it goes away."

Lucy stared at me, waiting for me to say more, but I didn't know what else to say.

I looked down and started walking toward the booth again. I had *so* not been prepared to talk about this, and I didn't want to talk about it anymore. Maybe later. No, on second thought, how about never? I'd be just fine with never talking about it.

Lucy seemed to have decided to let it go for now as we walked. We didn't quite make it to the booth, which was no big loss in my mind, but I wasn't too thrilled with what stopped us.

"She doesn't look so powerful," A petite, yet curvy woman noted, looking me up and down. Her dark, curly hair was styled to perfection, not an spot of frizz in sight. A small smile played across her cupid's-bow mouth. "I don't see what they're all so worried about."

She stood in front of us, flanked by two average sized men, one that looked to be somewhere in his thirty's, and the other looking maybe eighteen.

I knew that none of them were the ages they looked. These were the vampires Jason had met with last night. I hadn't seen their faces, but somehow I just knew. Maybe my supernatural radar was getting better.

A low growl trickled from Lucy's throat. I tried to hide my surprise at the sound. Apparently Lucy could tell what they were too. She probably smelled them.

"Now now," the younger looking man soothed in a cultured English accent. "We mean you no harm . . . today."

The young guy's dark hair was cropped close to his scalp, making his big blue eyes look even bigger. He'd look like a baby forever. Had to suck. I might have even felt bad for him if he and his friends weren't trying so hard to intimidate us.

Suddenly Jason was at my side, and Chase was beside Lucy. "We agreed you'd leave her alone Maggie," Jason practically growled, his eyes on the woman in front of us.

"No," Maggie corrected, good cheer dripping from her words. "We agreed that I would not kill her just yet."

"A little sure of ourselves, aren't we?" I chimed in, feeling more than a little peeved.

Every little ounce of good cheer leaked from Maggie's small round face, as if it had never been there at all. "No one was asking for your opinion little one."

Little one? I had to be at least five inches taller than her. "Listen shortstack," I replied. "You want to mess with me, you do it directly and to my face. If you haven't got the guts, then be on your merry way."

"Xoe," Jason scolded sharply.

I felt heat coursing through my veins. It probably wasn't smart to mess with a pack of vampires, but my temper had to come out one way or another. In this case, words were better than actions.

Maggie laughed, not realizing what could happen if I lost my temper. "Jason dear, you better keep your dog on a leash . . . and I'm not referring to the werewolf."

Maggie turned her attention from me and

walked a few steps to stand in front of Jason. She put a hand seductively on his chest. "I had almost forgotten how nice you are on the eyes Jason dear. I'm not quite sure what you're doing with *this* one." she remarked, gesturing at me with her eyes.

Jason grabbed Maggie's wrist and looked at her with an unexpected amount of hatred. I had never seen a look like that on Jason's face before. That look let me know that there was *a lot* of history between him and Maggie, and most of it was bad.

Maggie ignored Jason's hand on her wrist and placed her free hand on his chest as well. She leaned her body in towards his, but she wasn't looking at him, she was looking at me.

That did it. My mom had always told me to be the bigger person in these types of situations. People could only get to you if you let them.Well, obviously I was letting Maggie because I felt a hot wash of rage pour across me.

Jason, predicting what was going to happen, turned to try and grab me, but it was too late. I had a split second to think better of things and tried to turn my anger away from Maggie, but with power coursing in, all sense left me.

My vision went completely red. I could no longer feel the sun on my face or the gentle breeze. Faintly I heard Jason talking to me in a soothing voice to calm me down. Next thing I knew, I *was* calm. I was calm, and Maggie's dress was on fire.

One second she was there with a mixture of shock and hatred on her face, the next she was simply gone, running to put out the fire most likely. Some of the people around us gave us strange looks. They might have caught a glimpse of fire, but Maggie was gone too fast to cause much alarm. They were probably wondering less about fire, and more about the woman that just disappeared into thin air, leaving a faint burning scent in her wake.

Maggie's cronies gave me identical looks of amusement, and maybe a little bit of respect.

"You're very likely going to regret that," the young looking one said.

I shrugged. "You have no idea how often I hear that."

With that, they both ran off after Maggie.

"Xoe!" Jason snapped. "You have no idea what it took me to ensure your safety from her. Now you've gone and put all of us in jeopardy."

I sighed, feeling my last bits of anger leaking away. "I'm used to jeopardy," I replied.

"Jeopardy I can handle, but I'm not going to stand around and be talked down to by some random idiot, vampire or not."

Jason stared at me, shocked by my attitude or my actions, I didn't know. Probably both. Lucy had a similarly stunned expression on her face.

Chase grinned from ear to ear. At least someone found me amusing.

# Chapter Thirteen

The car ride back was just as much fun as the art market. That's some more sarcasm there, if you didn't catch it.

Jason drove, I sat in the passenger seat, Lucy and Chase both sat in the back. The tension was palpable. Lucy and Chase were both being quiet. This argument was for Jason and I alone apparently.

"We need to go home," Jason muttered, finally breaking the silence.

I stared at him a moment before answering. His jaw was set in a tight line, holding back a lot more emotion than he was showing. His fists were clenched on the steering wheel at ten and two. I knew he was only angry because he was worried, so I avoided my normal grumpy approach.

"We can't leave, we came here for a reason."

Jason didn't respond, but Lucy did. "We can leave Xoe. Forming a pack isn't worth risking our lives."

I sank down in my seat sullenly. "Who said anything about risking lives?"

Jason risked a glance at me to see if I was serious. I pointed out to the road to signal he should watch what he was doing. His reflexes were good enough that he could probably divide his attention without a hitch, but I didn't really want his attention on me at the moment.

"We risked our lives the moment we set foot in Utah," Jason began. "We knew you'd be challenged, we just assumed it would be by werewolves. Now not only do half of them want you dead, but Maggie does too."

I could pretend I wasn't afraid all I wanted. Heck, most the time it even worked. I have the uncanny ability to ignore fear until I actually believe that is isn't there. Though all it takes for me to be reminded is someone I trust telling me I'm acting like a crazy person. Jason knew all of this, and now it was his turn to bring me back to reality. We were armpit deep in alligators, and most of it was my fault. Now everyone wanted to give up and go home.

If we went back home, we'd continue to be in danger. At least being part of the werewolf community would add a certain threat to messing with us. It's one thing to take on something scary, knowing that if you kill it, nothing is going to come back to bite you. It's quite another thing to know that taking out the scary thing will only lead to the rest of the scary things coming after you. Yeah, we needed the pack. I'd rather risk our lives now, then have to look over our shoulders for the rest of them.

"We can't leave," I announced.

"Xoe-" Jason began to argue.

I raised my hand. "No. I know I've screwed us five hundred ways to Sunday, but it doesn't change why we're here. We have to risk it if we ever want to feel safe."

No one responded. That was agreement enough for me. We could all argue later, it didn't change the fact that we were staying, or at least I was.

We pulled up the the inn and parked. As we walked towards the entrance Jason stopped me.

"We'll be up in a minute," he announced.

Lucy and Chase hesitated, but at a nod from me, they walked away.

Jason grabbed my other arm and turned me to face him. He stared at me until I gave him direct eye contact. My heart felt like it was trying to beat it's way out through my throat. He was leaving. I knew it. I'd put him through too much, and he'd finally had enough.

He pulled me into a sudden and tight hug. "I can't have anything happen to you. You don't need to be part of this," he whispered into my hair.

I pulled away from him and held him at arm's length. "Come again?"

He pulled me closer, so he could whisper and I'd still hear him. "Your friends will understand. Lucy, Max, and Lela can all find packs here. They'd need to move to other areas, but they would be safe."

I shook my head. "Even if I were willing to leave them, I'm better off with a pack too."

He touched the side of my face gently. "Why do you think that?"

I met his earnest blue eyes with as much weight as I could put in my gaze. He looked so worried. He just wanted to protect me and I wasn't letting him. I *couldn't* let him.

"You don't get it," I explained. "I'm a rarity. You said it yourself, vampires would want to kill me just to taste my blood. Werewolves want to kill me because I'm a threat. We found out the hard way that witches want to kill me to see if they can steal part of what I am. I don't have a pack of demons to run to. If I don't do this, I'm alone."

Jason shook his head. "You're not alone. I've been by myself for decades. We could leave together. I'll take care of you. No one can hunt you down, if no one can find us."

"And when I get old, and you don't, and you leave me," I muttered. "I'll be all alone. What will I do then? Make new ties and start looking over my shoulder again?"

Jason looked completely taken aback. "That's what you think?" he asked.

I shrugged and looked down. "That's what's logical."

Jason put a hand under my chin and forced me to meet his eyes again. "You do realize, you might not even be mortal?"

I smiled bitterly. There was a small chance that I wasn't mortal, but I didn't really want it. I wanted to live and die with my friends and family. My dad was hoping for the small chance. He'll live forever if no one kills him. He doesn't want to watch his daughter die. Demons with a decent amount of human blood are pretty much a toss-up. Some of us aged and died like humans, some didn't

Really, I'd probably get killed off before I found out either way, so I hadn't put too much worry into it since I found out about that little chance.

"I probably am mortal," I argued. "And

it doesn't matter anyways. I'm not abandoning everyone."

I tried to walk away, but Jason pulled me back. "You're still not listening Xoe. By taking this route, you're putting all of them in more danger than they have to be. They're in danger because they're associated with you."

That stopped me cold. I hadn't thought of it like that. I was the freak of the bunch. As far as the entirety of the supernatural community was concerned, werewolves were a dime a dozen. I made us stand out. Standing out was not a good thing. He was right. Damn him, he was right.

I felt the realization slip across my face. "What will I tell them?" I asked.

Jason's mouth was set into a grim line. "The truth. I will never leave you Xoe. It's going to be okay."

Chase chose that moment to come trotting back outside. His pace slowed as he saw our expressions. Jason's arms dropped and I pulled my arms in to hug myself. For the first time in months, I felt cold.

Chase took one look at me and turned to Jason. "What did you say to her?" he demanded.

Jason glared back at Chase. "She needed to understand. It's her decision to make."

Chase stood closer to Jason, eye to eye.

"The choice to run away?" he asked coldly.

"It would keep her safe," Jason argued.

"It's *her* choice Jason," Chase said sternly. "It doesn't matter what we think of it, or what we'd have her do differently."

This had obviously been discussed beforehand without me. I wedged myself in between the two boys, facing Chase.

"I can't put everyone in danger anymore," I explained.

Chase looked down at me coldly. "They're in danger anyhow. You know I was against this plan, but you were right at the start. It could save everyone. They want you saved too Xoe."

"Wait," I started. "Has *everyone* discussed this without me?"

Chase took a moment to read my face before he answered. "Everyone agrees that this is the best thing. You're not the only one that gets to do the protecting Xoe. Your friends want to protect you too."

I hadn't considered that everyone else would be trying to protect me too. It wasn't just me taking care of everyone.

I had a thought. "So does Abel."

Jason walked around me so he could see my face as well. "What?" he asked.

I smiled. "Abel offered me his

127

protection. Technically I think that means he has to help with the vampire problem."

"What are you talking about?" Chase asked.

"Abel offered me his protection earlier, and I accepted," I explained. "The vampires aren't just going up against me, they're going up against Abel, and in effect, everyone he leads."

"But what difference does that make?" Chase prodded. "Maggie could slip in and try to kill you and run before any help would come."

I shook my head. "It's going to be a little difficult for her with werewolves hunting her down."

Jason looked hopeful. "Do you believe Abel would do that?"

I shrugged. "He wants this to work. He won't hunt her down himself, but I'll bet you anything I hold dear that he'll order others to. Maggie might think twice when she sees that messing with us means being hunted by the masses."

Chase smiled. Jason smiled. Why protect each other, when someone else would do it all for us?

# Chapter Fourteen

When we got back to the hotel room, Allison, Lela, and Max were still out doing werewolf activities, and my dad was waiting for us.

At the raised eyebrow he gave me as I entered the bedroom, I simply shrugged.

"Did you really have to light the vampire on fire?" He questioned.

"She had it coming," I mumbled in response, surprised that he already knew.

My dad chuckled, shoving his blond hair out of his face that eerily resembled mine. "We've been working on your control for just this reason," he lectured. "Have you been doing your exercises?"

My dad had taught me meditations to calm myself down when I was about to lose it. He made me practice them all the time, claiming that once they were like second nature to me, I'd do them automatically, and therefore wouldn't lose control anymore.

"I've been a bit busy," I replied.

Ignoring me, my dad turned his attention to Chase, who was still standing behind me near the door. "Chase?" my dad questioned. "Please make sure that she runs through her exercises every day."

Chase sat in on most of my lessons, even though his demon powers were nothing like mine. He just seemed to enjoy watching for some reason.

Chase grimaced. "I'll try."

My dad raised his hand and I knew he was about to puff out on us. "Wait!" I exclaimed.

He lowered his hand back down.

"I have two questions. First, Abel mentioned something about me not really knowing my demon history. Second, Abel offered me his protection, and I don't really know what that fully entails."

My dad raised his eyebrows again. "First Alexondra, neither of those are actual questions. Second, I am surprised at Abel's offer, but it could be highly advantageous if you're willing to swallow a little bit of pride."

I smiled. "Well I already swallowed it and accepted, so tell me my advantages."

My dad smiled back, his mouth a perfect

130

mirror of my own. It really is freaky how many physical similarities we have.

"Well," he explained. "The first advantage goes to me. I was going to arrange you some extra protection, but now Abel will obliged to do so instead. The rest of the advantages go to you. Once you publicly announce his *ownership* over you, anything that happens to you will be perceived as his fault. If you are hurt, it will be seen as the fault of his weaknesses, and not yours. A leader does not want to appear weak."

"So," I began, trying to put things together in my head. "I really gain a lot from this, and he stands to lose a lot. So why would he even offer?"

My dad sat back down on the bed to explain. "One reason could be that it will greatly improve your chances of forming a pack. If the other wolves see you cowed to their leader, they will not view you as such a threat. You will become a controlled element. Still, it is a big risk for him to take, which means he wants you under werewolf law very badly."

I shrugged. "He told me he wants demons linked to his faction of wolves so that they'll be scarier than the other factions. People are made more wary where demons are involved."

My dad steepled his fingers together in thought. "A very good point Xoe. So either he is a very good leader, risking a great deal for the continued safety of his people, or . . . "

"Or . . . " I prompted.

"Or he wants something else," he finished.

My dad shrugged gracefully. "I will do my best to find out, but the point is, you've already agreed. The wheels are already in motion, so we must simply make the best of the situation."

With that, my dad snapped his fingers, and was gone with a whoosh of fire and a poof of smoke. I realized he hadn't answered my question about demon history. I was willing to bet that he hadn't forgotten that I'd asked.

Chase moseyed a little closer to me. "Shall we?" he said with a sweep of his arm.

I eyed him suspiciously.

Chase raised his hands in an *I mean no harm* gesture. "Lessons? I just got a pretty good scolding for your lack of studying motivation."

"Right now?" I groaned, then looked at Jason for help.

Jason shrugged, he looked like he was thinking way too hard about way too many things. "I'd say you need all the practice you can get."

I gave my loving boyfriend what I imagined to be a truly terrifying glare.

Jason smiled in response. "Am I wrong?"

No, he was not wrong. I held onto my glare though. I turned to go into the other room with Chase when a motion from Jason stopped me. I signaled for Chase to go on and walked back to regard Jason.

Jason looked down with a dark look on his face. "I've known Maggie for a very long time," he admitted.

"And?" I questioned, not seeing the point.

Jason sat on the bed and pulled me down to sit next to him.

"I met Maggie shortly after I was turned," he began. I was instantly nervous. Jason never talked about his past. "We were together for a long time," he went on.

I raised my eyebrows. "Like, *together*?" I questioned, feeling a little shocked.

I mean, I'd guessed Jason had had a past, but I'd never tried to learn too much about that particular aspect. Just because he was my first real boyfriend, didn't mean that I was his first girlfriend. I felt sick, and I hated that I felt it. Past was past. Yeah, tell that to the little pit of rage boiling in the bottom of my stomach.

"Yes together," he admitted. "But I didn't love her, like I love you," he added quickly.

Isn't that what all boys say about their past relationships to their current one? You're different, special. I choked back bile. My reaction was so stupid. This was years, and I mean *years* ago. We're talking double digits here.

When I didn't speak, Jason continued, "She was old back then, I'm not sure how old, she would never tell me. She's much stronger than me."

I stood to make my way to the adjoining room. I didn't need to hear all of this.

"Xoe?" Jason questioned from behind me.

I turned partially to face him. "I'm not mad," I assured. "I just need to . . . process."

I waited long enough to see his nod, then quickly shut myself inside the girls' room. Chase and Lucy were sitting at the foot of Lucy's bed looking at the rest of the schedule of events.

Chase raised his eyes to me. "Everything okay?"

I nodded somberly and sat on the other side of Lucy. "I take it you heard?" I asked her.

She nodded. "Sorry Xoe."

I shrugged and turned to Chase. "Still up for running through my lesson with me?"

Chase hesitated. "So we *are* staying then, right? We're going to see this pack thing through?"

Lucy perked up at that before I could answer. "But Xoe," she began

I patted my hands at the air in a calming gesture. "There will be no more discussion Lucy, we're staying. Which reminds me, we need to get a message to Abel."

"After the lesson," Chase interrupted. "I don't need another lecture."

I glared at him. I'm not a big fan of my lessons. They're not bad, just boring.

"Fine," I replied crankily, eliciting a relieved smile from Chase.

Lucy sat awkwardly between us for a moment, then asked, "Can I watch?"

I shrugged. "Sure."

Chase and I moved to sit cross-legged on the floor, facing each other with our knees almost touching. It was usually me and my dad sitting this way while Chase sat off to the side.

It didn't surprise me when he started running through the lesson exactly as my dad did . . . he'd sat in on enough of them.

"Hold out your hands," Chase instructed.

I held both my hands out, palms up. Chase placed his hand palm down on my right hand. His hand was dry and slightly cooler than mine. He nodded at me, signaling that I should make a flame in my free hand. Having someone touch one hand helped me concentrate on making a singular flame in my other hand, don't ask me why. I guess instinctively I tried not to burn them, even though Chase wouldn't get burned anyhow. I could still light his clothes on fire though.

I closed my eyes and focused. I could sense Lucy sitting quietly on the bed. I focused on my free palm. I felt the surge of energy I always feel before I make a flame. I kept my eyes closed for a minute, focusing on sustaining it.

"Um Xoe . . . " Chase began.

Sensing the worry in his voice, I opened my eyes. I had made a flame like I was supposed to, but it was . . . huge. It was also a deep crimson color, as opposed to my usually natural orange flames. I stared at the flame in shock. It was incredibly freaky . . . yet beautiful. I'd never seen fire that color.

I took my free hand away from Chase. The stone on my ring was swirling with seemingly violent, unnatural lights. "You see it this time?" I asked Chase, holding my ring out for him to see.

"Uh huh," he observed nervously.

I for some reason wasn't nervous. I felt calm, if slightly awe-struck. I closed my hand that held the fire and it disappeared. There was no smoke in its wake like there usually was.

Lucy came to kneel beside me. "I take it that's not what usually happens?"

Suddenly a crash came from next door. We all instinctively bolted toward the other room. Lucy was the first to make it there, throwing the door open wide before rushing inside.

The vampires were back, and they'd brought friends. Maggie had a new dress, pastel pink with little flowers on it . . . ick.

"There you are," she observed upon seeing me.

Jason was being held back by her cronies that we'd met earlier, while an elderly woman with pure gray hair and another woman that looked eerily like Maggie stood watch. The Maggie doppelganger was in the exact same dress as Maggie, only in baby blue. Double ick.

"Maggie no!" Jason shouted and kicked out at his captors as she rushed me.

Lucy side-tackled her before she could reach me. Maggie threw Lucy against the wall like she weighed nothing. Maggie pinned Lucy with her hand on her throat. I watched in shock as Lucy started sputtering for breath, her hands clawing at Maggie's around her neck.

In unison, Chase and I grabbed Maggie and ripped her off of Lucy. Before I could see if Lucy was breathing Maggie turned on me and threw me to the ground, face contorted with rage. She looked nothing like the cute, petite woman I had seen earlier. She got a grip on my throat much like she had with Lucy, except she was straddling me to help pin me down.

Chase was there, about to pull her off of me, until he disappeared in a blur of motion with the Maggie look-alike on top of him.

My vision was going gray. I couldn't remember how to fight back. I felt something with my left hand as I flailed my arms feebly. I wrapped my fingers around the rooms' big heavy bible. I didn't know who had taken it out of the drawer but I was grateful. With a quick muddled thought that this was strangely ironic in some way, I swung the bible up to make a sickening crunch against Maggie's nose.

She fell back, losing her grip on my throat and Jason was suddenly there. He grabbed Maggie by her torso and threw her into the wall like she weighed nothing. The wall shook with her impact.

My senses started to come back to show

me chaos all around me. The wolves in the other rooms had to hear it, but no one came running to our rescue. Maggie came rushing back towards me, blood dripping steadily from her nose. I scrambled backwards to get out of her reach, but she was on me in seconds. She was faster than Jason, faster than anything I was yet to deal with.

I shoved my palm into her nose, making the blood flow more heavily, as she grabbed at my waist and dragged me under her. She managed to pin my wrists, hard enough that it felt like my bones might break. Her grip felt like an iron vice. She put her face right above mine and smiled.

The blood from her nose dripped near my mouth and into my nose. I sputtered as I kicked my legs to try and buck her off, but it wasn't working. I could hear struggles all around me, but everyone else was out of my line of vision. I tried to concentrate and form the same fire I had formed only moments before, but nothing was happening. My powers work with anger, not fear.

There was a giant thud at the door, and Maggie paused to look in that direction. A moment of silence and another thud sounded. One more thud and the door splintered and swung violently inward to slam against the wall.

Abel stood framed in the doorway for a moment, then he was just a blur of motion running towards Maggie.

Abel full on jump tackled her and they flew into Jason and the elderly woman, who had obviously been struggling with each other.

Maggie slipped Abel's grip and regained her footing to face him, but then something drew her attention to the other end of the room. With a blood-curdling scream she rushed towards Chase, who was crouched beside an unmoving Maggie doppelganger.

I didn't have time to wonder at the power suddenly flowing through me. Rather than forming fire in my palm, I closed my hands and focused on Maggie. Like magic, Maggie was on fire for the second time today. Except now I wasn't just being pissy. She was going after Chase with some serious intent. She'd just tried to strangle me. The calm realization came over me that I wanted her dead.

People always seem to think that they could never wish death on another person, but let those people watch the lives of their loved ones at risk. Let them come to the horrifying realization that someone they care about is about to die right there in front of them. Let them feel that perfect cool rage at those realizations, then ask them again if they're capable of wishing someone dead.

The acrid smell of burning flesh filled the room, then diminished as Maggie leapt right through the window, already shattered from the vampires' entrance. She wouldn't die. She was a vampire, a super old one. She'd heal surface burns in a matter of hours. Too bad.

I turned around just as Abel snapped the elderly woman's neck. I shuddered and wished I hadn't turned around so soon. Abel gave me a look of what seemed like respect. I was getting that look a lot lately. Apparently supernatural beasties only respected you when you punched them or lit them on fire, though I highly doubt Maggie's emotions at the moment ran anything near respect.

Maggie's other two cronies had bolted. Some friends they were. I wasn't sure when they had left, probably when they realized that we were putting up more of a fight then they thought us capable of.

Lucy was blinking and looked confused, like she had just regained consciousness. Despite the bruises forming on her throat she seemed okay. Jason was mostly unharmed, fancy that. Either vampires didn't like to hurt their own, or Maggie still had a soft spot for Jason after all of these years and had ordered him unharmed. I was betting on the second.

I went to crouch by Chase, who was still crouched by Maggie number two. His shoulder was bleeding. It looked like the woman had bitten him and torn a chunk of flesh away. His shirt was torn and very, very bloody. Blood was dripping down to stain the carpet.

I reached out as if to touch the wound, but let my hand fall before I could complete the action. Chase met my eyes, pain showing clearly on his face. "It's fine," he said shakily.

With wonderfully numbing shock coming over me, I looked down to who I had to guess was Maggie's twin sister. Well she had been her sister. Crap, sisters made into vampires? She had two perfect little puncture marks on the side of her neck. Dark yellow and green lines flowed under her skin, radiating from the bite and mottling the color of her otherwise pristine neck.

I turned back to Chase and he smiled feebly. I smiled back, don't ask me why. Chase is part Naga. He's poisonous. I'd forgotten that little tidbit. I don't think I'll forget again.

"Can you stand?" I asked him.

He started to nod, but then stopped with a wince of pain. He was a demon, he'd heal, but it still hurt.

I grabbed his hand and helped him stand. Jason and Lucy were both staring at us. Jason had a tortured look on his face, blaming himself for everything, as he often did.

Lucy looked pale despite her olive skin. She turned to go to the door, mumbling something about getting away from this mess, but I stopped her with a hand on her arm. I highly doubted that Maggie was waiting outside, but Lucy had been stolen from us once before, I wasn't about to risk it happening again.

Lucy stared at my hand like it was something foreign, and I withdrew it slowly. I looked down at my hand wondering if there was something wrong with it.

"How are you calm right now?" she asked.

I shrugged. Surprisingly I did feel calm. You could only suffer through so much action before you started to compartmentalize. I found myself wondering if it would all just suddenly catch up with me eventually.

Lucy shook her head. "The look on your face Xoe, you wanted to kill her. He," she pointed at Chase, "killed that woman. She's on the floor dead right now. Does it not register with you that there are bodies on the floor?"

I guess Lucy had been conscious for more of the fight than I'd thought.

"Lucy," Jason began, trying to stop the coming argument.

I shook my head and held up a hand for him to stop. "She tried to kill you. She would have hurt Chase."

Lucy squinted like she didn't understand, then shouted, "No one needed to die!"

"*We* would have died!" I shouted back, frustrated. "What part of that do you not get, Lucy?"

Jason finally cut in at that point. He came to stand in between me and Lucy. Chase just stayed leaning against the wall, bleeding and unsure of what to do.

I looked up into Jason's pain filled face. He didn't try to blame me for being ready to kill Maggie, or for the death of her sister. He just stood there looking miserable.

I tried to smile at Jason reassuringly, and he managed to force his mouth into a small smile back. Had he cared for Maggie's twin? He'd been with Maggie for years, so he obviously knew her. It was all a bit too much for me to deal with at the moment.

I stepped around Jason and Lucy, and led Chase toward the bathroom to clean his wound. I spared a glance at Abel. The elderly woman was crumpled at his feet, but he didn't seem to care. I shook my head and kept walking.

I left the door open behind us and made Chase sit down against the edge of the sink.

Without a word, I grabbed the bloody fabric of his shirt and finished the tear that had been started there. I ripped the shirt completely off of his arm so I could lift it over the rest of his body with him only having to move his good shoulder.

At a loss as to what to do with the bloody fabric, I settled for stuffing it into the bathroom's small trashcan. Chase watched every move I made, as if he'd memorize the entire sequence.

Suddenly uncomfortable, I turned towards the sink to wet a washcloth. Never having cleaned a wound before, I decided to start small with the bloody skin around the missing flesh. He'd already almost stopped bleeding, so I just had to clean up the blood that hadn't been absorbed by his shirt and jeans. I patted the skin around the wound and glanced down at the jeans again. The jeans could stay bloody, no way those were coming off while I was around.

"That's not your blood on your face, is it?" Chase asked.

Crap, Maggie's blood was still on my face. I quickly grabbed another towel and started scrubbing at my face in the mirror.

"It's not my blood," I answered. A sudden, horrible thought dawned on me. "I can't get anything from vampire blood, right? Like, nothing bad can happen?"

Chase gave me a weird smile. "Well, as far as I know, vampires don't carry blood-borne diseases. You probably couldn't get one even if they did, since your blood is far different from a human's. Also, demons can't become vampires, even if just getting some vampire blood in your nose could cause someone to become a vampire. I think you'll be fine."

I started to feel a little silly for asking, but hey, I hadn't known any of that stuff, so now I did.

Chase was still staring at me. I put down the bloody towel and looked at his wound again. "I'll get the first aid kit," I announced nervously.

I never used to carry a first aid kit around with me, but somehow I knew we'd need it at some point . . . imagine that.

When I entered the bedroom, Jason was sitting on the edge of our bed with his face in his hands. Lucy was sitting beside him silently, refusing to look at me. Abel was on his cell phone, murmuring to someone quietly.

Jason looked up when he realized I'd entered the room. "Xoe, I'm so sorry-" he began.

I smiled weakly. "Later, okay?"

He nodded then looked down at the

elderly woman's body still crumpled where Abel had left her. I was leaving that one to someone else. I was not in the business of hiding bodies. Maybe Abel would do it. He'd done if for us before.

I realized I still had some of Chase's blood on my hands. My clothes had soaked up some too from helping him into the bathroom. I wiped my hands on my jeans, then proceeded to shuffle through my suitcase. I found the first aid kit at the bottom and stood to go back into the bathroom.

"Is Chase okay?" Jason questioned weakly.

I nodded. "He's fine. We'll all be fine."

I went back into the bathroom without another word.

Chase was standing, examining his wound in the mirror. He didn't look pale, and seemed cognizant enough, so I assumed he hadn't lost a dangerous amount of blood. Demons may be tough, but they can still die from blood loss, just like anyone else.

I pushed him gently to sit back down. "Stop messing with it," I lectured.

Chase smiled, but then his smile quickly faded as I soaked a cotton ball with rubbing alcohol. "No way!" he exclaimed.

I put my free hand on his good shoulder

and met his eyes. "Now now," I soothed. "Be a good boy and you'll get a lollipop afterward."

"It'll heal fine," he argued.

Not listening I began to dab the cotton ball on his bite. She'd really done a number on him. Even with his increased healing abilities it would take a while. There was just too much flesh missing.

Chase let out his breath at the initial sting, but didn't complain any further. Only when I really started focusing on the wound, did I realize that yes, I was staring into a big gaping hole in someone's shoulder. I started to feel dizzy.

Before I could stop myself I swayed to the side. Chase reacted before thinking of his pain and raised both his arms to catch me around the waist. He pulled his arms back down when the pain hit and I went down.

I ended partially leaning against Chase's chest as I tried not to hurt him, while at the same time I tried in vain to get to my feet. Some blood had pooled on the floor, preventing me from getting enough traction to stand. I kept slipping back down and landing on Chase.

Someone cleared their throat from the doorway behind me. I braced myself and turned. Devin had his hand over his mouth to hide his smile. Great, just great. I hadn't heard him come

148

in the room. Jason had propped the nearly shattered door back in place while I was cleaning Chase's wounds, so I would have heard him moving it to come in.

Chase finally got his good arm around my waist and helped me stand with him.

Devin grinned, no longer trying to hide it. "Did somebody call room service? I'm told we have a body or two."

Abel must have called him, and I was grateful for it. I really didn't want to see the body again.

I squinted at Devin suspiciously. "How did you get in?"

"Abel let me in through the adjoining room," he explained, still trying to hide his laughter. "I thought you might be hesitant to open the door to this room. Now about the bodies . . . "

I pointed out into the main room. He knew that was were the bodies were, he just wanted to give me grief. After Devin walked away, I realized that Chase's arm was still around my waist. He squeezed me a little closer and I felt blood soak into the bottom of my shirt. I might have been mad if it wasn't already ruined anyway.

I stepped away. "I need a shower."

"Thanks for doctoring me," he replied.

"Any time," I mumbled.

He nodded, a small smile playing across his face.

I was just so damn amusing today.

# Chapter Fifteen

I left the bathroom to find Devin and Jason wrapping the elderly woman's body in a rug. That's right, they were seriously wrapping her up in a rug. A second rug had been procured and Maggie's sister was already wrapped up tight. Jason and Abel lifted the ends of the now rolled up rug with only a little visible effort and walked it into the girls' room.

Abel didn't even have to put down his end when he used one hand to grab the knob. The door shut behind them, and I heard another door open and shut as they went out the girl's room and into the hallway. I wasn't sure where they were going with the bodies, it looked pretty darn suspicious, but I figured they had it covered.

It was my turn to go into the girls' room so I could shower. Before I went through, I had a thought, and I turned back to regard Devin as he gathered up the other rug all by himself. "Tell Abel he's doing a bang up job on *protecting* me so far. I might just have to reconsider the whole deal."

Devin's eyebrows raised. "So that's why he was here?" he questioned. "He offered you his protection?"

Apparently it was a secret. Oh well.

"Yes," I answered, "and I took it. Now tell him to do a little better."

Devin smiled politely, something changed in his demeanor and I didn't know what or why. "Of course, I'll get the message to him right away."

I really should have just gone into the other room already, but letting things go is not one of my strong points. "What does Abel offering me his protection mean to you?"

Devin smiled again, the picture of a perfect gentleman, except for the corpse burrito in his arms. "Nothing, nothing at all."

He was lying, but short of threats I couldn't really make him tell me anything. I took a deep breath and went into the girls' room without another word.

Lucy was sitting on the edge of one of the beds. Lela, Max, and Allison still weren't back. I imagined rumors would be circling soon enough and they'd find their way back to our rooms in a hurry.

"Is Chase okay?" Lucy asked.

"Fine," I grumbled. I grabbed my forgotten shampoos and headed into the bathroom.

I wasn't sure if Lucy deserved my grumpiness, but my adrenaline had faded and I felt like crap. She probably deserved it . . . maybe. I'd think about it later. I just wanted a few minutes alone.

As I had suspected, my clothes were completely ruined. I felt dizzy for a moment thinking about how all that blood had come out of Chase. I sat on the edge of the bathtub to try and steady myself. As I sat I peeled my bloody shirt off and tossed it into the trashcan.

I stood and turned the shower on, then finished undressing. My jeans wouldn't fit into the little trashcan so I put them in the sink.

After stepping in, I waited for the shower water to run from pink to clear before I shampooed my hair. Ick. I had blood stuck under my fingernails, and I couldn't quite seem to get them clean.

I gave up on my nails and finished showering. Then I got out to find that I once again forgot clean clothes, only this time I was way too tired to care. I wrapped a towel around me and ventured out into the bedroom.

Everyone was huddled in the girls' room, making it seem smaller than it already was. My suitcase had been placed right outside the bathroom door. I crouched down and picked out some new jeans and a plain white tee-shirt. New bra and undies, and back into the bathroom I went.

I got dressed and came back into the room to find several newcomers. The newcomers in question were dressed in all black, two men and one woman. Their attire and stance practically screamed bodyguard.

"Let me guess," I said sarcastically. "You're here for our own good."

I got three curt head nods in response, all in unison. Well at least Abel had chosen to take his job seriously. I decided to ignore our new friends and regarded the old ones so that the inevitable questioning could begin. Lela, Max, and Allison had to have already heard the story from those that were there, but they apparently needed to hear my perspective.

After my recap everyone went silent.

"Why are we all in this room?" I asked.

Max shrugged. "Chase bled all over ours. They're cleaning it."

I looked at Max skeptically. "Who's they?"

"The inn's staff," he replied.

"Apparently they know."

I looked to Lela for confirmation.

She shrugged. "The entire staff is one type of supernatural or another. I thought you guys knew."

I narrowed my eyes at her. "How would we know."

Lela held up her hands in surrender. "I'm sorry, but it's kind of obvious if you paid attention."

I shook my head. "Whatever."

I looked around at the room, everyone was staring at the floor dejectedly as if the world had ended. Chase had put on a blue plaid, button up shirt over his bandages. Jason wouldn't meet my eyes.

I turned away from them all to search the room for my purse. I found it on the night stand by the room's phone. I tossed it over my shoulder and headed for the door.

"Where are you going?" Lucy called from behind me, a tinge of anger in her voice.

"Dinner," I replied curtly, not bothering to turn around. "As soon as you guys are done wallowing, you're welcome to join me."

Max was by my side in a split second. We were out in the hall and about to shut the door, when Chase raced out to join us.

I raised my eyebrow in question at him.

"I don't think you're in much shape for bodyguard duty."

Chase shrugged, then winced at the pain. "Jason seems to think you don't want to be around him right now."

I couldn't argue with that. Hell hath no fury and all that . . . but had I really been scorned? I didn't think so, but I was pretty set on acting like I was.

I was hoping that by leaving the room we would escape the bodyguards, but there was a whole other set of them waiting outside the door. I mean, I was grateful for the extra protection and all, but it felt weird having strangers watch us. The bodyguards fell into step behind us without a word. I felt like patting them on the head and saying, "good bodyguards" but I'd probably lose a hand.

I continued down the hallway without another word. Max, Chase, and the bodyguards followed in my wake. We walked down the stairs and past the semi-upscale restaurant that was part of the inn. There was no way we were eating in there.

I almost made it to the front door of the lobby. I was *that* close, when I noticed Darla walking towards us. Her tight curls had been braided back away from her perfectly sculpted face. She was still in the same clothes she had worn earlier, and I realized with a start that I had just met her that morning. It seemed like days ago.

She came to stand before us with arms crossed. Instead of acknowledging anyone else in the group, she just looked directly at me and asked, "Where are you going?"

I smirked up at her. "None of your damn business."

She sighed loudly like I was wasting her time, when really she was the one that was wasting mine.

"Did you need something?" I asked snarkily when she didn't speak again.

"Abel wants to speak to you in private," she said, frustration coloring her voice.

I raised an eyebrow at her, but she simply turned around and started walking away. I almost didn't follow her, but thought it might be stupid not to, given that he'd just hidden two bodies for me . . . even though one was his fault.

Darla went into a conference room and shut the door behind her, either assuming that I'd come in behind her, or not really caring either way. I'd go with not caring.

I peeked in the little window to make sure Abel was actually in there, and it wasn't some sort of trap. He was there, and I was surprised to see that Devin wasn't.

"You'll all wait right here?" I asked our little group.

Chase's mouth was set in a stubborn line. "I'd rather come in with you."

I sighed. "You know that's just going to delay the process. He's going to try and make you leave, and then we're all going to have a nice argument about it. Finally you'll leave, because I actually do want to hear what he has to say."

Chase nodded, clearly not happy, but it was good enough. I went into the room and shut the door behind me.

Abel and Darla were already sitting on the far end of the long conference table. Without being asked, I walked over and sat down across from Darla with Abel in the end seat.

"I would like to hammer out the details of our arrangement," Abel announced. "I want to make sure you understand everything Alexondra."

I nodded. "Sounds good to me, though I'm not fully understanding why Darla is here . . . no offense," I added, looking at her.

Abel smiled and put his hand on Darla's. "Darla is my wife," he announced.

"No shit?" I asked loudly, genuinely surprised. "Doesn't that make her like, co-leader?"

Darla chuckled. "Not exactly Xoe. Werewolf hierarchy is extremely chauvinistic."

"What, is it like a law?" I asked them, feeling grumpy at the idea. Stupid werewolf politics.

Abel shook his head. "Not a law really. Our traditions spring from pragmatism. We fight to become leaders. Men win more fights. Of course, not all men are bigger and stronger than women, but if you take a group of people, the one biggest and strongest person is most likely a man.

"That's why you don't see many female leaders. Female alphas within a pack sure, but for there to be a female pack leader, she would have to be able to physically take on every man in the pack. It happens of course, but just not that often."

I wrinkled my eyebrows in distaste. "Sounds stupid."

Darla laughed. "Tell me about it. What they don't get is that most of us are smart enough to stand back and let the men take the beatings for us. I could kick this man's ass any day of the week," she said, gesturing with a thumb at Abel.

Abel simply smiled and gave Darla's hand a squeeze in return. It was weird seeing him in this element. All happy and . . .

domesticated.

"We're getting off topic," Abel announced. "On to the matter of your protection. I assume you've told your father Alexondra?"

"For the last time, it's Xoe, and yes I told him," I answered.

Abel steepled his fingers in front of his face with his elbows on the table. "And what did he think?"

I shrugged. "He's not sure of your motives, but he thinks it could be beneficial."

Abel smiled. "Alexondre, ever the pragmatist."

It still weirds me out to hear people say my dad's name. Not only do we look freaskishly alike, we also have almost the same name. My mom really dropped the ball on that decision.

Abel seemed to be thinking for a few minutes, then finally spoke. "We'll need to make an official announcement, but until then, my protection of you is no secret. If anyone threatens you in any way, you let them know exactly what they're dealing with, as well as alerting me immediately. I'd rather not get jumped unawares by a group of vampires."

I hadn't really thought of things like that. Abel was really sticking his neck out for me. For some reason though, it didn't make me feel any more trusting. In fact, it just made me more suspicious.

"Also, you need to wear this," he added handing me a bracelet of braided blue leather cord. The braids were extremely intricate, with the individual cords dyed different shades of blue and blue-green.

"Um, no thanks," I said, as I tried to hand the bracelet back to him.

Darla held up her wrist to show me the same blue bracelet. "Just wear it," she ordered. "It won't hurt anything but your pride, and the other wolves will know what it is. You won't have to go out of your way to tell them you're under Abel's protection."

I took the bracelet reluctantly, but couldn't tie it around my wrist one handed, so Darla reached over the table to help me. Her fingers were long and nimble, and the bracelet was tied in a complicated looking knot in seconds.

I stared at the knot. "Well now I'll never be able to get it off."

Darla smirked. "That's the point. You need to keep wearing it after you get home. You're representing the coalition in your area now. Any traveling wolves will make note of your standing."

"They're not going to be looking to me

for leadership or anything right?" I asked, needing reassurance.

"They will not." Abel answered. "They may however, give you a message if they wish to relay something to me."

"And they don't have phones?" I asked sarcastically.

Abel laughed abruptly. "We're not barbarians Alexondra. They would simply trust someone under my protection to give me a message, more than they would my secretary."

I raised an eyebrow. "You have a secretary?"

Abel nodded, like it wasn't a big deal. "I am a very busy man Alexondra. I don't have time to take phone calls from every wolf that gets mad at someone in their pack. Serious calls are filtered through to me. I don't concern myself with the others."

"Well since you don't answer your calls, wouldn't it kind of defeat the purpose if I just had to leave their message with a secretary regardless?" I asked.

"You don't understand Xoe," Darla answered. "You being under Abel's protection makes you part of the, well I guess you could call it the inner circle, though that sounds a little dramatic for my taste."

"Okay," I went on, "so what you're

trying to say, is that I can bypass the secretary?"

"In so many words, yes," Abel responded. "You will be able to speak directly to me. If you feel there is a threat to you and yours, you must notify me right away."

This was getting complicated. There were probably a million more questions I should have asked, but I was hungry, and I didn't feel like chatting anymore.

I sighed loudly. "Anything else? Is this where you teach me the super secret handshake?"

"We'll teach you the handshake later. First there is the matter of the tattoo . . . " Abel began.

I jumped up out of my chair, knocking it to the ground. "No way!" I shouted, crossing and uncrossing my arms like an umpire. "There is *no* way you are branding me!"

Abel and Darla erupted into laughter, and I realized that they were screwing with me.

"Sorry," Abel responded, laughter straining his voice. "I just couldn't resist."

I crossed my arms across my chest grumpily. "Are we done now?"

Abel nodded with tears streaming down his face. That's me, Xoe Meyers, everyone's favorite source of amusement.

# Chapter Sixteen

I walked out of the conference room with a sour expression on my face. Chase and Max were sitting on a couch against the wall with a bodyguard standing on either side of them. I noticed the other bodyguard standing by the lobby's front door, watching everyone like a hawk.

I stomped over to the couch. "Ready?"

"I take it the meeting didn't go well?" Chase asked.

"It was fine," was my reply before turning to walk towards the lobby door.

Max and Chase got up to follow me, and the bodyguards closed in to flank us like a black cloud. It was unnerving as hell, but I grudgingly admitted to myself that it did make me feel safer. Though the main source of comfort was knowing that Jason and the others had their own pack of bodyguards with them in the room.

As we continued out the door, I pulled the SUV keys out of my bag. We walked across the lawn, then all piled into the vehicle silently. I was officially glad for the vehicle, since it fit the three of us, and the three bodyguards. Though now that I was out of the inn, I had no idea where I intended to go.

I decided we'd just drive down the main drag and look for a place to eat. I found one pretty quick, a brick-oven pizza place with a sign that said they sold burgers and stuff too. Something for everyone.

I pulled in and parked. "This okay?" I asked the other passengers, gesturing at the restaurant.

"Well you did already park," Max said sarcastically.

I grimaced. "Sorry, it's been a long day."

"Ok," Max said simply, seeing my logic and forgiving me. If only all arguments could be so simple.

We got out of the SUV and walked into the restaurant. We were seated quickly in a booth that was all wood with no cushions. It was meant to look rustic, but what it really was, was uncomfortable.

The bodyguards refused to sit and eat with us, and instead stationed themselves strategically around the restaurant, one by the door, one by the bathroom and one seated in a near-by booth.

Chase sat next to me, and Max sat across from us. We decided on sharing a pizza with all of the fixings. Upon ordering, I remembered how much Max could eat, which was an absurd amount given his size, and added on an order of pasta with Alfredo sauce to share on the side.

We got our drinks, water for me and Chase, soda for Max, and then it was just the three of us.

"So what's with the bracelet?" Chase asked, looping a finger through the offending object on my wrist and lifting it up.

I shrugged, trying to not act as bothered as I actually was. "It's a sign of Abel's protection. Apparently all of the other wolves will recognize it, and know what it symbolizes."

"And it symbolizes . . . " Chase began. "Abel's ownership?"

"Like a dog collar!" Max laughed.

I blushed in spite of myself and pointed a finger in Max's face. "Hey buddy, I'm doing this so Abel will protect *all* of us. See these fancy bodyguards all around?" I asked, gesturing to the figures in black. "They're here, because I'm wearing *this*," I said, putting my bracelet in his face.

Max raised his hands in mock defense. "Calm down," he said, still laughing. "Please don't light me on fire. You know we all appreciate what you're doing."

I smiled and finally laughed at myself a little. I crossed my arms and turned my nose up at Max. "Darn tootin'," I responded haughtily, then added, "Maybe I'll get you a bracelet too so you don't feel left out."

"Oh pretty, pretty please?" Max asked jokingly bouncing in his seat like a little kid.

I smiled. "Well see. If you're a good boy, we'll get you a pink one."

"My favorite!" Max exclaimed, just as the waitress came and sat our food on the table along with three plates. After asking if we needed anything else, she walked away.

Chase shook his head. "I don't know what I'm going to do with the two of you," he said playfully.

"You're going to eat with us, duh," I responded tartly.

We all quickly filled our plates. Out of our complete group, the three of us are the ones with the biggest appetites. Ordering the pasta was definitely a good idea.

"So why is Lucy mad?" Max asked, mouth full of pizza.

There it was, no building up to it, no

warning of intent. I didn't really know why Lucy was mad. I knew why she was bothered, and maybe a little uncomfortable, but all any of us had done was to protect her and everyone else.

I shook my head and swallowed my bite of pasta. "She's upset because of what happened with the vampires that ended up in our rugs. She's also upset that I would have put Maggie in the same place if I'd had any choice."

Max stared at me for a heartbeat. "Why would that make her mad?"

Hallelujah, I wasn't the only one that didn't get it. "I'm not sure, really. I would love for someone to explain it to me."

We both looked at Chase, and he shrugged. "They would have killed us. I don't see what the big problem is."

I found myself wondering just what Lela's viewpoint was. For some reason, I thought she'd side with us. Lela was a lot of things, and one of them was a survivor. She did what she had to do. Maybe we could make teams and have a nice little debate on the topic.

"How's your shoulder?" I asked turning towards Chase, changing the subject.

He shrugged, then winced. "It would be fine if I didn't keep forgetting there was a chunk torn out of it."

"It's healing okay though?" I prompted.

"In a few days I'll be right as rain," he replied.

You gotta hand it to supernatural healing. Out of the three of us, Chase actually healed the slowest, even though he had more demon blood than I do.

Both of his parents were demons, so he got demon blood from both sides, whereas I only got it from my dad. The difference is that my "demon line" is more powerful, hence better healing. Max heals even faster than I do. Werewolves are freaky like that.

"That raises another question," Max interjected. "What the heck did you do to that vampire Chase?"

Chase looked down, embarrassed. "You didn't tell them?" he asked me.

I shrugged. "When you told me, you made it seem like it was for my ears only."

Chase smiled. "I appreciate that."

Max was staring at us with his mouth open in mock annoyance. "When you two are done grinning at each other, could one of you please answer my question?"

I blushed and looked down. "My mom was a Naga," Chase explained.

Max raised his eyebrows. "What the heck is a Naga?"

"A snake person," I answered as if it was

common knowledge. "like in Hindu mythology."

"So . . . " Max prompted.

"I'm poisonous," Chase answered.

"*That*," Max began, "is So. Cool. So what happens when you make out with chicks? Do they die?"

Chase laughed. "No Max, they do not die. My fangs are retractable."

"So unlike our little Xoe here," Max joked, "You probably won't accidentally kill your mate of choice."

I frowned at him. "I'm yet to kill anyone by accident, thank you very much. You better just hope I don't start with you."

"Speaking of our choice in mates," Chase said to Max, "care to enlighten us about your brief stint as Allison's suitor?"

"Yes Max," I added, fluttering my eyelashes at him. "Do tell."

Max shrugged as a blush crept up his cheeks. "She's cute, and I like how she's all bossy, so I asked her out."

"She might be cute," Chase answered, "but that girl is scary."

"Aw," I cut in. "I thought *I* was the scariest girl around."

"You're scary because you can light things on fire with your mind, and you're

171

beautiful to boot," Chase said casually. "Allison is scary because she has absolutely no doubt of her ability to get her way, no matter the situation."

Max laughed at Chase's analysis. I was stuck on him calling me beautiful. Had it been a slip up? I didn't think so. He didn't seem at all embarrassed about saying it.

"I guess I like 'em confident," Max replied. "Though it becomes a major personality flaw when the confident person wants to become a werewolf."

We sobered up a bit at that.

"I'm not going to let her do it," I stated.

"You may not be able to stop her for long," Chase countered.

I frowned, thinking about Allison.

"Oh, shut up and call her beautiful again," Max said loudly. "Her expression was a lot better then, than it is now."

Chase finally blushed. "I was simply stating a fact," he explained. "Xoe is a scary beautiful demon with a penchant for destroying household appliances."

I was still thinking way too hard about things, but we all laughed and went back to our food. We managed to finish every scrap of food, and have an uneventful dinner, complete with witty banter and entree sharing.

Imagine that.

After dinner we reluctantly drove back to the inn. I found myself once again thinking about just giving up and going home. I missed home. What I wouldn't give to just lie down in my bed and feel safe again. I hadn't felt completely safe in a really long time.

It wasn't really the werewolves that had caused problems, though many of them had been quite unpleasant. I had a bad feeling we hadn't seen the last of Maggie. Honestly, she didn't seem all that scary to me. Sure, she was super strong, and super fast, but who wasn't around here? Yet she came with friends, and we'd just killed her sister. Grief can fuel a lot of rage. Rage gets people dead.

Chase, Max, and I walked across the front lawn, bodyguards in tow. We all stopped at the same time.

Things seemed unusually quiet around the inn. Like way too quiet. As in, there was no one. Anywhere. In the words of Scooby Doo, "Ruh Roh."

# Chapter Seventeen

Max and one of the bodyguards trotted ahead into the inn. They came back out quickly. Max shook his head. Gone. We'd left Jason, Allison, Lucy, and Lela in the room. Chase tried to grab me as I bolted. They couldn't all be gone.

I slipped his grip and made it to the front door. Max followed me inside. I assumed Chase wouldn't be far behind. The bodyguards stayed on the porch. Apparently we'd fallen outside of their job description.

I frantically climbed the stairs to our floor, not willing to wait on the elevator. The inn was completely deserted, not a single sign of life. I went in through the girls' room, since that was where we'd left everyone. It was spotless. The beds were made, and everyone's luggage was gone, including mine.

Numb, I went to sit on the nearest bed. I was too afraid to check the other room. I knew what I would find. Max entered the room, shortly followed by Chase. They each came to sit on either side of me on the bed.

"What's going on?" Max asked, voice shaky.

I turned to look at his elvish face, usually filled with good humor to find a single tear sliding down his cheek. I hadn't gotten to tears yet. I knew they would come in time if we didn't figure things out.

Chase put his arm around me. I could smell the blood from his bandages. "We should keep looking. If we can't find anyone, we need to leave. Waiting here won't do any good."

I nodded and stood up slowly, letting Chase's arm drop from my shoulders. I stumbled as I started to walk to the door and Max caught me. It took me a second to regain my footing. I felt like I was in a dream. I looked down at my ring and it was dead, no signs of swirling lights.

When we reached the lawn, the bodyguards were gone. Gre-at. The sky was blue and perfect. It seemed wrong given the circumstances. Something was going on, some kind of . . . magic.

"We can't get out!" Max called from my left.

I turned to look at him, he was pushing at thin air like there was something solid there. I walked cautiously to the edge of the lawn. It got harder to breathe the closer I got. I raised my hands, and there was . . . something. Not a wall exactly, it felt more like static. Static so thick that we couldn't push through it.

Chase came to stand by my side. He lifted his hand up beside mine, then slowly let it drop.

"It's some kind of magic," he said, shaking his head.

Max came to stand at my other side. "I found the bodyguards."

I looked a question at him. He looked green. Rather than answer with words, he pointed. I followed the direction of his finger to the inn's front porch. We'd run right past them. Well, what was left of them.

Even from the distance I could tell they were no longer . . . intact. Blood dripped in a steady flow down the wooden slats. It was one of those train wreck moments where you wanted to unsee everything, but instead you walk closer to find out all of the details.

We stopped walking about ten feet away from the corpses. Ten feet was more than close enough. A foul odor seeped up from the pile. I'd always heard that fresh death came with an ugly smell, especially when someone is cut up enough that the fluids and other matter inside are exposed to the clear blue sky. I turned away quickly and lost my lunch. Max wasn't far behind me. Chase managed to keep his cookies.

I spit a few times to clear the taste of bile out of my mouth, then stumbled farther from the bodies to sit in the grass.

Chase came to stand beside me. "We have to try to get out."

I tried to summon a flame into my hand. Maybe if I could make a flame large enough I could throw it at the magical barrier. My hands didn't seem to want to work. I had a sneaking suspicion that I was going into shock. I couldn't get my magic, or ability, or whatever you wanted to call it to work.

Max sat down, far to my side but still in my peripheral vision. He was obviously trying to not interfere as I stared at my hand like it was a tool that was broken.

"Why aren't they coming?" I asked no one in particular.

"Who?" Max asked.

It took me a minute to realize what he'd asked. Yeah, definitely in shock. "Whomever killed the bodyguards. Why are we still alive?"

"Do you guys smell that?" Max asked, ignoring my question.

I was pretty sure that my question was a lot more pertinent, but I answered, "I've been trying not to smell too hard."

Max shook his head. "I couldn't smell it before, all I smelled was the bodies, that's why I noticed them. It smells like musty stone. Like a cave."

I took a whiff. I smelled moisture, like the smell before it rains, but there was something different about it. Max was right, it smelled like a cave, or somewhere underground.

I closed my eyes and focused on the smell. Once I focused on that, I felt cold. The grass beneath me felt like stone. I opened my eyes and the sky was gone.

"We're not in Kansas anymore," I mumbled. Then I realized I had no one to mumble to. I was mumbling alone in an empty stone cavern. I wasn't alone for long.

# Chapter Eighteen

She was preceded by a rather wicked cackle. First I saw torchlight. There was other light in the cavern, but I couldn't tell where it was coming from. Maggie came prancing around the corner, torch in hand. She'd swapped her floral dress for a black one. It flowed past her knees to meet with knee-high black boots. I wouldn't have chosen stilettos for stomping around in caves, but then again, I hadn't chosen to go stomping around in a cave to begin with.

"Oh little girl," she chimed. "Did you really think it was a good idea to stand up to a vampire."

My laugh was harsh and dry, and probably sounded more like I was choking. "You didn't do this on your own. You don't have that kind of power."

She cocked her head. "Don't I?"

I looked her dead in the eye. "No, you

don't. Where are my friends?"

She laughed. "Oh you don't need to worry about them. Well, at least the ones you left at the *real* inn. I still care a little for Jason after all of these years. I might just have to explore those feelings more, once you're out of the way."

Ignoring her not-so-subtle prod, I asked, "What about Chase and Max?"

She shrugged. "Them you might have to worry about. If they ever manage to think their way out of that fabricated reality, they'll just end up down here, and I assure you, I'm not the only bad thing in this neck of the woods."

I smiled bitterly. "I'm assuming the one that actually created that reality is down here? I'd say that wolf is probably much bigger and badder than you."

She smiled back, but not like she was happy. "We are far better than wolves my dear. Though yes, he is down here somewhere. I'll have to have a word with him. It should have taken you longer to get out. I was so enjoying watching your confusion. By the way, you reek of vomit."

She'd walked close enough that I spit at her, wiping the smile off her face. Now she could smell like vomit too. Surprisingly my gesture didn't cause her to attack me . . . yet.

Her smile returned quickly. "Remember how you couldn't arouse your magic in that other reality? You can't do it here either. I wanted to show you just how weak you are. I wanted you to realize your inferiority before I killed you."

I smiled again. "You know, you're the third psychopath that has lectured me before you killed me. Yet, here I still am. Can't say the same for the other two."

I was bluffing. I was screwed without my magic. I'm stronger and faster than a normal human, but nowhere near as strong and fast as a vampire. She either had a demon or a witch helping her. Since we were in a creepy underground lair, I guessed demon. They had a weird penchant for creepy underground lairs. Not that the realization helped me any.

"So what did you offer the demon that helped you?" I asked, throwing her off guard.

Her smile faltered again. Yippee. "That, little girl, is none of your concern."

It was my turn to smile. "No, I guess it's not, but it *should* be your concern. I think you should be concerned with getting out of here after you kill me. I think you should be concerned with the fact that a demon would just as soon eat you as send you merrily on you way."

"I'm not afraid of demons."

I laughed. "No Maggie, you're not afraid of me, or maybe you are, seeing as you went to all of this trouble to magically neuter me. This demon had the power to create an alternate reality that trapped two demons and a werewolf. I'd say maybe this demon is a little scary."

Maggie sneered at me. "I have a deal with him. I'll be home safe and sound as soon as I dispatch of you."

"If by home," I replied, "You mean the burning fiery hell pit in which you belong, then yes, you will be there very soon."

An anger filled, "Enough of this," was the only warning I had before she rushed me. I stood and tried to dodge out of the way, but she was too fast for me. She grabbed me and used her momentum to toss me in the air like a rag-doll.

I smacked into the stone wall with a thud, and slid into a pile of rocks. I looked down in horror when I realized that amongst the rocks were bones. Most of them had been either shattered or gnawed to little stumps. I tried to pretend that they were animal bones, but I knew I was fooling myself. The teeth on that jawbone looked a little too human.

My left shoulder throbbed from the impact, but I was otherwise numb. I was guessing numb was a bad thing. Numbness after getting hurt usually meant either your body was yet to register the pain, or nerves were damaged. I was probably hurt a lot worse than I could feel.

Maggie stalked towards me. The only way she could tower over me was if I was on the ground, so that's where she'd put me.

"You brought this all on yourself," she spat down at me. "You had to be a snarky little twit. You could have just walked away."

I smiled and felt something wet drip down my face. I realized it was probably blood, but I ignored it. "Now Maggie," I lectured. "If I had walked away, you would have just been more jealous when you realized that my butt is way nicer than yours. You would have probably tried to kill me on the spot."

I was going to die, but I'd be damned if she had the last word. Suddenly Chase materialized behind her and tapped her on the shoulder. She whipped around in surprise and I took the opportunity to kick her just below her right kneecap. There was a loud crunch and she went down.

Before I could blink I had her dainty little fangs inches from my face. Chase grabbed her hair to hold her back as she snapped at me like a rabid dog. The leg I had kicked was bent at an odd angle, but she didn't seem to feel it yet.

Like a slow-motion horror scene, her snapping jaw inched closer to my face. I fumbled around in the pile of rocks and bones until I wrapped my hand around a large stone. I promptly smashed that large stone to the side of Maggie's skull.

She fell away from me, but within seconds turned on Chase, screaming unintelligibly about him killing her sister. He fell back with his right arm raised to keep her teeth away from his throat and she started worrying at his arm like a starving animal. For the second time today Maggie was seconds away from doing some serious damage to Chase. I didn't want to do what I was about to do, but I couldn't quite stand up to help him, so I was doing it anyway.

"I want to make a deal!" I called out.

Maggie paused and faced me with blood running down her mouth and neck. "What are you doing!" she snarled.

I ignored her. "Oh big powerful demon!" I called. "I think I can offer you much more than some little vampire!"

Maggie lunged at me as another form materialized in the cavern. He was Friggin. Huge. He had to be around 6'7" and built like a tank. His skin was the darkest color I'd ever seen on skin, so dark that it had purple and blue highlights. His eyes were black, and not just the pupil and iris, the entire eye.

He grabbed Maggie mid lunge like she weighed nothing. She was left dangling from his grip on the back of her dress. "We had a deal!" she screamed, enraged.

Ignoring her, the demon turned to me. He smiled. His teeth were pointed. "What kind of deal, little one?"

"Um," I began, glancing at Chase. He was cradling his bloody arm to his chest. He gave me a *what are you doing?* look and I turned back to the demon. "First I have to know what Maggie offered you, then I'll better the deal."

He smiled again. He smelled like rotten meat. I was pretty sure I knew who had killed the bodyguards. He spoke in a surprisingly cultured voice. "She offered me her vampiric lackies to run my errands up top." He looked at the ceiling of the cavern, which really wasn't that far from his face. "Those of us unlucky enough to have no trace of human blood can only go up top when summoned."

Did that mean my dad had some human blood? I'd think about that later, if there was a later. My dad was going to have to sit down and tell me all of the information I was lacking. I really didn't appreciate getting into so many life or death situations without knowing the rules.

"Do you know who my dad is?" I asked, trying to buy time.

The demon started swinging Maggie back and forth like a toy. "I grow tired of your games little one," he replied.

"My dad is Alexondre. Do you know him?" I pressed.

The demon chuckled. "Oh Alexondre, he used to be so much fun back in the day . . . until he started sullying himself with that human woman. I was unaware there were any offspring."

I bit my tongue before I said something I would regret in response to him insulting my mom. Instead I said, "So you're friends? You and my dad?"

The demon let Maggie slump to the ground, but still kept a hold of her. "I said I knew Alexondre, not that we were friends."

"Well, wouldn't it be nice to have him owe you a favor?" I asked hopefully.

My dad probably wouldn't appreciate me bartering with his favors, but hell, he owed me too. It was time for him to pay up.

The demon eyed me skeptically. "What could Alexondre possibly do for me?"

Maggie started crying. I almost felt bad

for her. Then she started mumbling about how she'd see me and my entire family burn and I stopped feeling bad.

"Well, what would you want?" I asked.

"Xoe, don't do this," Chase interrupted.

The demon pointed a finger back at Chase. "*You*, are not in this conversation. Your bloodlines are so mixed up that I feel tainted even being near you."

"Just keep me here and let Xoe go," Chase blurted out. "I'll do your errands. I can come and go easier than vampires."

The demon turned to look at Chase. Maggie struggled as he dragged her across the floor, then gave up and went limp.

"I believe I said you were not in this conversation," the demon lectured. "Speak again and I'll kill you."

This was going nowhere. There was obviously one thing that the demon really wanted. "What if my dad and I could find a way for you to go up top whenever you liked?"

"Xoe stop!" Chase shouted.

The demon smiled again. "Little one, if I could do that, I would never come down here again, but I fear it is not possible."

Crap, I didn't really have anything else to bargain with. It really probably wasn't possible.

189

"Let us try," I pleaded, ignoring Chase. "and if we can't, then I'll run your errands personally."

He showed me his pointed teeth again. "Done."

"We had a deal!" Maggie screamed, as she began to thrash around in the demon's grip.

I got to my feet and shakily walked to where Maggie dangled. My legs and back still felt slightly numb, so standing at all was a major feat.

"Little girl," I chided.

Maggie went still and met me with scared eyes. I almost felt sorry for her . . . almost.

Chase came to stand beside me, shirt soaked in blood. He smiled, even though he was a little too pale and *so* was not happy with the situation.

"Hasn't anyone ever told you," he continued for me.

"Not to make deals with demons?" we said in unison.

I couldn't help but think that Chase was lecturing me as much as he was lecturing Maggie.

The large demon chuckled, then promptly tore Maggie's heart out of her chest. I was going to be sick again.

# Chapter Nineteen

"My name is Bartimus," the demon explained, "but you may call me Bart."

Just when I thought I'd heard everything, now I was meeting Bart the demon.

Bart had manifested a small cafe table and a teapot with two cups. Chase wasn't allowed to sit at the table. He was sulking in the corner. Bartimus looked even more massive sitting in his little wrought iron chair.

I sat in the other small chair and Bart poured us each a cup of tea and took a sip of his. Our tea came from the same teapot, so I grabbed mine and took a sip. Hopefully this wasn't a *Princess Bride* type of situation and I was about to die of Iocaine poisoning. The tea tasted like cinnamon.

"You never told me your name little one," Bart prompted.

"It's Xoe," I answered.

"Not just Xoe," he argued. "That's not your full name, I can tell."

"How?" I asked, suspicious.

"Little Xoe, my powers are of the mind," he explained. "I can create other realities. Little white lies don't get by me. Due to this, I also know you have no intention of actually helping me."

"I would be a fool to break a deal with a demon," I countered.

"Yes you would," Bart agreed, "but you hope that since you and your father are demons as well, that you can get around that little rule."

I shrugged, feeling ill. "It was worth a shot."

Bart grinned, and the stench of rotting meat dripped from his mouth over the scent of the tea. I was about to get eaten. I was totally going to get eaten. I started to stand.

"Calm down little one," Bart chided. "I'm not going to eat you. I would not eat Alexondre's only child. That would be barbaric."

I relaxed thinking that Bart was the last person I'd expect to not do something just because it was barbaric.

"I'll simply need a vial of your blood," Bart said as if it was the most common thing in the world to say.

"No," Chase said very firmly as he stood.

Bart stood as well and walked toward Chase. Chase stood his ground. Bully for him, he was still about to get himself killed.

"I'll do it!" I shouted. "If you tell me what it's for."

"No, you will not," came a voice from the other side of the cavern.

Bartimus whipped around in surprise, then smiled. "Alexondre! How lovely it is to see you!"

"What exactly do you think you are doing with my daughter?" my dad asked, a grim expression on his face.

Bartimus grinned even wider. "Little girl made a deal with me," he explained.

My dad turned to me with one of those looks on his face that are reserved for the sole use of parents who are extremely disappointed in their children.

I looked down at my teacup. "I didn't really have a choice I mumbled."

"She really didn't," Bart agreed.

My dad turned to Chase. "Your job is to keep her *out* of trouble. You seem to have failed."

"Don't blame him," I interrupted. "He's already gotten munched on twice by vampires in

193

the line of duty."

Bartimus was practically bouncing up and down with excitement, for all the world like a giddy school girl. A giant, flesh-eating demon school girl. The image would have been comical if we weren't in such terrible circumstances.

My dad sighed loudly. "You're not taking her blood Bart."

Bart lost his grin. "Then how will I ensure her promise?"

"You won't," my dad explained. "There is no deal."

Bart raised a hairy eyebrow. "Do you really want to go there Alexondre? You may or may not be able to take me, but where will that leave our little Xoe in the meantime? Where will that leave her when I crush your bones?"

My dad had a sour expression on his face. "I give you my word," he mumbled.

"What was that?" Bartimus called out, grinning and cupping a massive hand to his ear. "I couldn't quite hear you, dear friend."

"I give you my word that I will do whatever Xoe has promised you," my dad stated clearly.

Bart snapped his finger and a long paper scroll appeared in one of his hands, and a feather quill in the other. The paper looked like a contract.

"Seriously, are we in a Disney movie or something?" I remarked.

Bart ignored me and thrust the contract at my dad.

"What did you promise him anyhow?" my dad asked.

I couldn't quite meet his eyes. "Um," I mumbled. "Just to help him gain his freedom to live in the human world."

"Oh Xoe," my dad sighed. "It *had* to be that."

Bart chuckled as my dad signed the contract.

My dad walked over and grabbed my hand without another word, while I stayed sitting in the chair. I wasn't sure if I could stand again anyhow. He signaled for Chase to grab my other hand, and Chase obeyed silently.

"Send us back up," my dad demanded.

"Can't get out yourselves?" Bart mocked.

"I know very well what type of wards you employ Bart," my dad grumbled. "Now send us back or our deal won't do either of us any good."

Bart grinned wickedly and snapped his fingers. I felt a sickening whooshing feeling in my gut, and clung to Chase and my dad like lifelines.

195

We ended up in the grass in front of the inn. My knees gave out as the world steadied itself around us, but Chase and my dad kept us upright. My dad let go of my hand as Chase put his arm around my waist to keep me on my feet.

I seemed to be struggling with a great deal of vertigo and my limbs remained numb. Chase finally hoisted me up into his arm and started carrying me towards the inn with my dad walking beside us.

A few werewolves in the lobby gave us weird looks and I managed to give them a little salute. They could gawk all they wanted. I'd take gawking werewolves over the empty alternate reality inn any day of the week.

The rest of our group was waiting for us when we got back. They were not exactly calm. Apparently they were the ones that had called my dad, so they knew he was coming to the rescue, but they obviously didn't have much faith in him, because we caught them in the act of devising battle plans of their own.

Jason ran to Chase and took me out of his arms. "What's wrong with her?" he asked.

"Vertigo," Chase explained. "Traveling by demonic means can be a bit much when you're not really used to it. Traveling from a warded demon lair is quite a bit worse."

"Will she be okay?" Jason prompted.

"I'm right here," I interrupted, looking up at him from the cradle of his arms. "I might also be injured, besides the vertigo. I'm not sure. Could you put me down now?"

Jason smiled, ignoring my grumpiness. He took a moment to hold me a little tighter, then placed me gently on the bed. I was starting to feel better and managed to sit up on my own. Jason scooted in close to me, and gripped my hand as if he didn't quite believe that I was actually there.

I leaned against him and let him support most of my weight. I didn't need the help sitting up, but just feeling him next to me again was pretty much the best feeling in the world right then.

I regarded the rest of our group standing around us. Lucy and Allison looked as if they just didn't know what to do with themselves. Lela was looking at my dad with a nervous expression on her face. I didn't blame her, my dad could be pretty scary.

I envied everyone their ability to stand. Standing would still take a little while. I was having trouble focusing on any one thing in the room.

I was able to focus well enough to see Max sitting on the edge of the other bed. "Glad to see you made it back," I commented.

Max glared at me. "I was stuck at that *other* inn with the dead body guards until about thirty minutes ago."

"Hey, it's not my fault you couldn't think your way out of it," I snipped. "The place we ended up was definitely not an improvement."

Max still looked cranky. I was guessing he was more upset that he couldn't get out of the other reality and Chase and I could. Bartimus must have freed him after he decided to deal with us rather than Maggie. Or maybe Bart just decided to stop putting any effort into the other reality, and Max was freed because Bart just didn't care. I was leaning towards the second option.

"So are you going to tell us what happened?" Allison prompted anxiously. "Max told us about the empty inn, but where did you and Chase go?"

I thought for a minute on the easiest way to explain it. "Maggie hired a demon to trap us. We ended up in his lair. The demon killed Maggie, now we owe the demon."

"Owe him what?" Lucy asked.

Jason pushed a little closer to me, if that was even possible. "Um, I began. It doesn't matter right now. We'll figure it out when we get home."

No one pushed me for more information.

I imagined I looked just as bad as I felt at that moment.

"Well I'm off to try and sort out this mess," my dad announced.

"How did you find us so quickly anyhow?" I asked before he could disappear.

My dad gave me a look like I was asking a silly question. "I couldn't sense you through Bart's wardings, but as soon as Max described what had happened, I knew where you would be."

That made sense, since he'd known Bart back in the day.

"Wait," I demanded again, when I saw he was still about to leave. "What are we going to do?"

"*We* will not be doing anything Alexondra," he replied. "I'm now contractually bound to figure out a way to help Bartimus. If it can be done, I'll have to do it, then I'll have to kill him. Bartimus cannot be released into this world."

"What would he have done with my blood," I asked.

"Bart can focus his power using someone's blood," he explained. "His mind games are strong enough without the extra control."

"Tell me about it," I mumbled.

There was a flash of flame and my dad was gone.

There was a knock at the door. No way. No more people. Hadn't I dealt with enough? Lela jumped into action and was at the door in seconds. She had barely opened it when Abel came striding in, followed closely by Devin.

Seeing me alive and well, Abel breathed a visible sigh of relief. "You are not making this arrangement easy," Abel grumbled at me.

I shrugged. "Sorry. Take heart in the fact that it sucks a lot more for me."

"Was it a demon that took you?" he asked.

"Do you really want an explanation?" I responded tiredly.

Abel furrowed his brow. "I don't. Not right now at least, but I do want to know if I have to protect you from demons as well as vampires."

I shrugged. "I don't think you'll have to protect me from a demon just yet, or any vampires for that matter."

Abel seemed to relax a little bit more. Devin raised his hand to hide his smile. I was yet to see Devin angry or upset. He always seemed amused. It was unnerving.

"The packs are getting ready to vote," Abel announced.

"*Now*?" I whined. "I *just* got back. How did you know anything was wrong anyhow?"

Abel glared at me. I was getting a lot of glares lately. "Three dead werewolves appeared suddenly at the front door, along with Max."

I opened my mouth to explain.

"No," Abel held up a hand. "Explanations can come later, you need to get ready."

I closed my eyes in frustration and Jason wrapped his arms around me. "Can't it wait?" he asked.

"No," Abel replied, then walked back out of the room.

Just then I noticed that Devin was holding a garment bag. "That better not be what I think it is," I said warily.

Devin gave me a truly evil look. "Abel is announcing his protection over you. Matchy matchy time. Werewolves do love a good show."

"Well shit," I replied, at a loss for words.

"Time to stand up and get ready," Devin prompted.

Stand up? Easier said than done. A demon's life is never easy.

# Chapter Twenty

The dress was midnight blue and strapless, with glimmers of tiny crystals visible along the bodice. I'd worn more dresses in the past days than I had my entire life. I wasn't starting to like it any more. In the end Allison and Lucy had helped me hobble into the bathroom to change.

Walking was getting easier, I just hoped the ability fully came back to me by the time of the vote. I had a feeling looking weak would not be a good thing. Plus it was frustrating as heck not being able to make my limbs work properly.

My back was a colorful speckling of healing bruises from being thrown against the cavern wall by Maggie. The dress showed all of the bruises on my upper back. Screw it.

I was sitting on the bathroom sink again while Allison worked on my face. I'd struggled at first, but I couldn't exactly run away. Lucy was sitting on the closed toilet seat.

Allison finished her work and I started to slide down from the counter-top. During my descent, the hem of my dress caught on the faucet. My feet met the ground and at the same time I heard a loud rip. I'd just gone and torn my dress. It was the straw that broke the camel's back.

"Screw it!" I threw up my arms haphazardly.

I stumbled out of the bathroom, completely fed up. I went and plopped on the floor by my suitcase and started pawing through my clothes. This was just all too much. I was done with stupid dresses. I turned my back to face the room and scooted the dress down off of my chest so I could put a bra on, then pulled my new dark blue *Les Mis* shirt on.

I forced myself to stand, bracing against the wall as I regarded the room. Max and Lela had turned to give me privacy. Allison and Lucy were standing just outside the bathroom door looking at me like I had lost my mind. Chase looked worried, and Jason's eyes were full of pity. I didn't want pity, but yet I couldn't help it as the first tear slid down my face. Jason walked up and took the jeans out of my hand.

I swayed as Jason searched for the dress zipper, then started working it down over my hips. Chase came to stand in front of me and gave me his arms for balance. Someone had bandaged his new wounds while I was holed up in the bathroom. He looked at my tear streaked face with a reassuring smile. Jason managed to get the dress off, then helped me step into my jeans.

"No more dress up," I said to Chase shakily.

He nodded. "I'm with you on that one."

No one else said anything as Jason helped me to the bed so I could put my shoes on. I was beginning to worry that I actually had nerve damage from being thrown against the wall.

Chase voiced my concerns out loud.

Jason nodded. "I was thinking the same thing."

"Will I be ok?" I asked, suddenly nervous.

Jason smiled. "You healed a broken bone pretty fast last year. You should be fine soon enough."

I let out a sigh of relief, making my ribs hurt. Allison came to stand in front of me with a makeup wipe. I'd probably screwed my mascara all to hell, so she graciously just wiped it all off.

"Let's go," I announced.

No one argued.

Jason lifted me back into his arms. "I'll

put you back down when we reach the lobby," he explained. "Then we can help you walk from there."

He pushed his way through the door with the rest of our group following behind us.

"Thanks," I replied.

"You're welcome," he answered.

"And Jason?" I asked.

"Yes Xoe?" he asked, smiling down at me.

"I love you," I answered.

"Get a room!" Max yelled from behind us, then started making loud gagging noises.

"I love you too," Jason answered with laughter in his voice.

Something started happening to my chest, and I realized I was laughing too. Imagine that.

# Chapter Twenty-one

Abel had gawked at my jeans and sneakers, but the vote was passed anyway. We were officially a werewolf pack. He had also announced his protection over me. There were some less than happy faces over that, but no one argued out loud.

We all made it back to Shelby in one piece. I was relieved to be home, though the looming problem of Bartimus was still on my mind. Allison was still a human, but now that we were home I knew she'd continue on her quest to become a werewolf. What she didn't know was that I'd put the kibosh on her plans.

I'd had Devin spread the word that anyone who dared try and change Allison would have to answer to me, and in effect would have to answer to Abel. I was still considering locking her in a closet though.

I knew it wouldn't be long before

Bartimus started pestering me about his release into our world, and Allison started pestering me about why the werewolves she met were unwilling to turn her, but I decided these were simply all problems for tomorrow . . . or maybe the day after. Today I would become reacquainted with my bed.

I sank into my pillows and thought about my mom. She'd hugged me when I got home, but didn't ask about the trip. She didn't ask if I was now the leader of a werewolf pack, or if we had been attacked by vampires and demons. It made me sad. I had always been able to talk to her before, and now she was too afraid to even ask what was going on in my life.

I couldn't help but be a bit angry with her too. I'd had to accept all of the things that were happening. I'd accepted that this was my life now. She was my mom, shouldn't she be accepting things too?

I was beginning to drift off, surrounded by the nest I had made out of my pillows, when a soft knock at my door startled me back into wakefulness.

My first thought was that maybe my mom wanted to talk after all. The door opened while I was still thinking about it, and Lucy and Allison came creeping into my room. I wasn't surprised to see Lucy. So we had a difference in morals with the whole killing people thing. What were a few scruples between friends?

When they saw me snuggled amongst my mass of pillows, they took one look at each other then made a running jump in unison. They ended up dog-piled on top of me until I tickled and pinched them away.

We ended up sprawled on my bed side-by-side, with me in the middle, breathing heavily and laughing.

"So how are you feeling, oh great and powerful leader?" Lucy asked.

I thought about it for a moment. "I feel ancient and tired, yet young and afraid at the same time."

Allison turned her head to look at me. "Wow Xoe, that was pretty deep for you," she said sarcastically.

I reached for a pillow and sat up so I could pretend to smother her. "Look away Lucy," I commanded. "You don't need to see this."

"Oh trust me Xoe," Lucy replied playfully, "I've been wanting to get rid of Allison for a looooong time."

Allison wrestled the pillow away from me and propped it under her head. "You two suck," she chided, but was smiling while she said it.

A throat cleared in the doorway. We all glanced up to see Max standing there with three pizza boxes in his hands.

"Oh please," he said, moving the pizzas to one hand so he could gesture with the other for us not to get up. "Don't let me interrupt the all girls pillow fight. I can wait."

Suddenly a pillow whipped across the room to hit Max in the face with a loud thwap. He almost dropped the pizzas in surprise. I turned to give Lucy a high five as we all erupted into raucous laughter. It felt good to laugh again.

Max stomped over to the bed and plopped the pizza boxes down at our feet. "Where are Chase and Jason?" he asked as he sat on the edge of the bed.

It was a good question. Jason and Allison had both left cars at the airport. Allison had taken Lucy, Max, and Lela home, and Chase and I rode with Jason. They had dropped me off first. I knew Jason was going home to unpack, but I hadn't thought to ask Chase where he was going. He'd had a hotel room before our trip, courtesy of my dad, but I had no idea if he still had it.

I reached across Lucy to grab my phone off of the nightstand and scrolled through my recent calls to find Chase.

He answered barely after the first ring

with a questioning, "Hello?"

"Where are you?" I asked, not bothering to explain my whole thought process.

"Umm . . . " he replied.

"You don't have a hotel room anymore do you?" I asked.

"Well, I kind of checked out when we left," he explained, "because I didn't know if I'd be coming back to Shelby. Now the hotel won't let me pay cash and I don't have a credit card."

"Did you call my dad?" I asked.

"I tried," he explained, "but he's down dealing with demons, trying to figure out what to do about Bart."

"So where are you now?" I laughed.

"Well," he answered. "I was sitting on a park bench, preparing to call you. Now I'm standing beside said park bench."

I laughed again. "Come over loser. Max bought pizza. I'm sure my mom won't mind you staying on our couch, and if she does you can stay with Jason."

I could practically hear him smiling on the other end of the line. "Be there in a sec," he answered then quickly hung up.

"Taking on a new roommate?" Allison asked sarcastically.

Before I could answer, Lucy shot Max a stern look. "Girl talk, get out."

Max feigned offense. "Oh come on, I already know that Chase is in love with Xoe."

"Did he say something?" Lucy demanded.

Max had an expression on his face that said we were all being extremely silly. "Oh come on," he answered, "no one had to say anything to me. It is *so* blatantly obvious."

"Yeah," Allison agreed, "But boys aren't supposed to be able to pick up on things like that."

"I'll have you know, I'm extremely perceptive!" Max argued as Allison got up and shoved him out of the door.

A few seconds later the downstairs TV turned on and the sounds of a soccer game filled the silence.

"So," Allison began, "Don't you think Jason is going to mind if Chase stays here."

I shrugged, feeling defensive. "Well then he can stay with Jason if Jason doesn't want him here. I don't really care, he just needs a place to stay."

Allison looked at me like I was being a difficult child. "This is *us* you're talking to Xoe, your life-long best friends. You can admit that you care . . . at least just a little."

"Fine I care . . . just a little," I answered. The front door opened and shut downstairs.

"Now everyone shut up about it."

We left my bedroom carrying the pizzas to find Chase watching soccer with Max. I plopped the box I was carrying down on the coffee table, then went into the kitchen to make some coffee.

I came back out with my oversized Edgar Allan Poe mug filled with coffee and lots of cream. Allison and Lucy had made Max move to the love seat with Chase so they could sit together on the couch and save me a spot between them.

I sat down and took my first sip of coffee. Feeling instantly better I asked, "Aren't you all sick of me yet?"

"Don't be silly Xoe," Max answered. "You're our wise and omnipotent benefactor."

I threw a pillow at him, almost spilling my coffee in the process. I had a feeling I'd be hearing jokes about me being their new leader for quite some time.

The front door opened again to reveal Jason, freshly scrubbed and dressed in a flannel shirt and jeans. I liked the flannel way better than the dress clothes.

Before he could walk in, a fire erupted momentarily behind him, quickly extinguishing to reveal my dad. Jason was unfazed by my dad's abrupt appearance. He simply walked inside then held the door for him.

My dad looked unusually disheveled. He was normally the picture of good hygiene, but now his gray dress shirt was missing a few buttons and had one sleeve torn off, and his face and clothing were covered either in ash or dirt.

"This Bartimus problem might be a bigger deal than I originally thought," he announced.

Did I mention that a demon's life is never easy?